sylvania
$ 23.95

Aliens of
Transylvania County

Patrick Bone

An Imprint of
The Overmountain Press
JOHNSON CITY, TENNESSEE

This book is a work of fiction. All names, characters, places, and events are either the product of the author's imagination or are used fictitiously. Any resemblance to actual events or persons, living or dead, is entirely coincidental and beyond the intent of either the author or the publisher.

For Gary and John

Best friends are hard to come by.
May we never grow up.

PROLOGUE

Beware the night,
When full moonlight
Gives parents cause to fear.
For on that night
Of full moonlight,
The children disappear.

Yes, you'll hear the winds a-howlin'
Like a baby child so dear,
A-wailin' like your baby cries
When evil stalks too near.

And you'll rush up to your darling's room,
And hold him close in fear,
On that dread-filled night
Of full moon bright
When the children disappear.

I KNEW THE LEGEND. Everybody did. Grownups wouldn't talk about it, except maybe on a full moon when they laughingly suggested their children not go out by themselves. But you could see it in their eyes. The fear. It hid in their eyes, and we saw through their laughter.

We kids believed the legend. We believed there were times over the years, on a full moon, when kids just disappeared.

I believed it, too, like I once believed in Santa Claus, and the Tooth Fairy, and Robin Hood, and. . . .

But it was 1956. I was a senior in high school, too taken— secretly, so that none of my classmates would know—with Davy Crockett and a new rage named Elvis, to be concerned about a scary children's story.

Then one night, on a full moon, I discovered children really did disappear from Transylvania County. I discovered how and why.

But nobody believed me. Worst of all, I would be the one to pull the short straw and wind up having to try to solve a mystery nobody wanted to admit.

PART I
Devil's Mountain

CHAPTER ONE

Well, I dare you,
Double dare you,
Triple dare you,
Yes I do.
Bet you'll never,
Never ever,
Do the things
That I will do.

HOW DO YOU SUPPOSE a fellow would be stupid enough to do something he knew all his life he shouldn't do? Take Devil's Mountain, for instance. We all knew it would be most near suicide to climb up that forbidden mountain at any time of the day or night, much less on a full moon. So, how do you suppose I was stupid enough to do just that?

I got into it all by myself. First time—and last—I agreed to smoke a hand-rolled cigarette. Schoolyard. Lunch break.

Wedged into a corner of the building where no one in authority could see us make fools of ourselves, we passed our forbidden weed to one another, wondering in our minds what could be so exciting about tobacco that it should be forbidden. But it wasn't the green on my face nor the nausea in my stomach that made me feel regret for having been there that day. Nor was it the terrible blackness that invaded my mind just before I lost my lunch. No, I would recover from that humiliation in due time.

What I would come to regret much longer was another dare I foolishly jumped upon during those same rebellious moments, when I was out of my mind from nausea and shame and jealousy.

John Croshaw started it all when he announced to me and my fellow conspirators, "I'm going up Devil's Mountain on the full moon. Bet you're all too chicken to go with me." He said it loud enough for the entire schoolyard to hear. But most of all, he said it to one particular girl who couldn't take her eyes off him.

He knew it. He knew she had a terminal crush on him. That's why he said it looking straight into her eyes. That's why he said it with a passion that all the rest of us could see, so we would know he meant the invitation for her and her only. That was John Croshaw for you.

I hated John Croshaw.

Actually, there were times he seemed like a good guy. He had an okay personality. Though he was new in town our senior year, he got along with most everybody. But I hated him.

I had to. Because Hannah Jane Goins—the girl I had loved from kindergarten, the girl I planned to marry, the only girl I could even talk to without stepping all over my tongue—had fallen totally and shamelessly in love with John Croshaw.

And she said, "Yes! I will go up Devil's Mountain with you on the full moon, Johnny."

The stupid things girls do for boys.

She called him Johnny. She smiled when she said it. His name tripped off her tongue like she had just tasted chocolate fudge.

I thought I would barf again, right then and there. But I didn't. Instead, I did something dumber. I said, "Me too!"

If it hadn't been for Hannah Jane, I never would have said it. Oh, if looks could kill, the one I got from John Croshaw would have been mortal.

The stupid things boys do for girls.

If only I had known then the consequences of my decision. But it was too late. Everyone in the group heard me say *Me too!* No turning back now. I had committed myself to an act for which I would pay, and pay dearly.

I wish I had puked again, indeed. It would have been easier on me than the nightmare that loomed ahead.

Not that I didn't understand how Hannah Jane could fall for the jerk. Handsome? No, he was not handsome. Handsome was too simple a word. He was, to quote Hannah Jane Goins, "Extremely fine!"

Extremely fine? I will allow she had a point. Next to John Croshaw, I didn't stand a chance. I was short, with brown eyes, brown hair, and a cowlick on the back of my head that stuck up only when I wanted to look neat. I tried hard to keep it down. Water wouldn't work. Just made it stiffer.

Once, I used some of the hair cream Daddy kept in the bathroom medicine cabinet. Wildroot Hair Lotion, it was called. *That's me*, I said, *wild roots*. If anybody ever had hair with wild roots, it was me. So I slurped it on my head, right up there on the back where my hair stood at attention. Know what? It worked.

For the first time in my life, I went to school minus Mr. Cowlick. Only problem was, I smelled like flowers. Lots of flowers.

It took the other boys a while, sniffing the air and making funny faces, before they figured out it was me. But when they did, they made the most of it, smelling the back of my head and saying, "You sure do have on great perfume today, Chester," and such as that.

That's right. Momma named me Chester, after her brother, Uncle Chester, the one who went to prison a couple of years before I was born. When kids were not making fun of me, they called me Chess. I liked that better. It would do, I decided, till I grew up and changed my name to something cool. Like Johnny.

Before I forget, the best thing about me was the gap between my two front teeth. Even in high school, I was remembered for my one claim to fame. An ability I inherited when my permanent teeth arrived. I could spit farther and with more pinpoint accuracy than anyone else in my class. A lizard on a log didn't stand a chance when I worked up a wad and let fly.

Back to John Croshaw. He was over six feet tall. Even for a senior in high school, that was tall in the '50s. He had sand colored wavy hair with no cowlick, and blue eyes "like a calm mountain lake." That's how Hannah Jane Goins described them to me during the hours she would spend telling me how extremely fine he was and how totally and eternally she loved him.

You see, Hannah Jane, in addition to being the girl I wanted to marry, was my friend. I always told myself, that was the real reason I agreed to join her and John Croshaw that night under the full moon.

The crazy part about what Hannah Jane and I did, by agreeing to go up Devil's Mountain on a full moon, was that we should have known better. John Croshaw was new to our part of the world. He wasn't raised with the most natural fear a kid in Transylvania County could have—Devil's Mountain. A black bear was less frightening than Devil's Mountain.

I knew for a fact that John Croshaw had heard the stories. He chose to ignore them. Worse, to make fun of them.

Naturally, as I was soon to discover, there was more to John

Croshaw than what met the adoring green eyes of Hannah Jane Goins. I imagine it was that adoration that muddled her judgment, for she knew better.

Of course, so did I.

Hannah Jane and I had reason to stay away from that mountain. A few of the braver kids had heard the real story from Momma Opalona, the black storyteller who lived down in the holler at the edge of our town.

Now that I think about it, Hannah Jane got me into that mess too.

CHAPTER TWO

Listen to the storyteller talk.
You don't come to listen,
It be time to walk.

HANNAH JANE GOINS got my attention way back on our first day of school ever. Her long, cinnamon colored hair and green eyes reminded me of a princess I saw once in a storybook. She was skinny then. She stayed skinny. Her bony knees made her legs look longer than they were. But I had to admit, from my point of view, she owned the neatest skinny legs in our class. And then she graced me with her smile. I had lost the war before the first gun had been fired. She would smile, and I would do anything she asked.

By the fourth grade, my love for her had matured. Seems she took to just about every boy in class, save me. I know, because she confided it all to me: her love interests, the boy she would marry—at least for that particular day or so—and the names of her future children. Most boys so rudely treated would have left for greener pastures. Not me.

I even made excuses for her behavior when Principal Gibson rang the school bell to signal our air-raid drill we always had to do to get ready for when the Communists dropped the atomic bomb right smack dab on our school. Hannah Jane made the experience a rewarding one for herself, the way she made a point of running over to where she could kneel on the floor snuggled up against whatever boy she had her sights on. The girl had no shame.

And my love knew no bounds. Someday, surely, I decided, my patience and hidden virtues would win her over. Besides, my qualities as a listener served Hannah Jane's need to expound quite well. She never had any problem starting up a conversation with me. She just loved to describe her newest challenges—which I took with a grain of salt, because she would always come up with yet another adventure before she had time to accomplish the previous one. So in the fourth grade or so, when she said, "Let's go visit Witch Opalona," I failed to take her seriously.

"That's *Momma* Opalona, Hannah Jane," I said. "My momma said she ain't a witch, and I should never call her one."

Hannah Jane didn't care what my momma said. "Witch Opalona? Momma Opalona? Don't matter to me, Chess. Let's go down the holler and see her, anyways."

Only the bravest—or most foolish—youngsters dared visit Momma Opalona's isolated shack to hear her tell stories. Everybody knew for a-certain that if the old woman did not like you, she would put a hex on you. All kinds of hexes, from tying your tongue to making you stutter. Warts were the worst. She gave you warts, you were in big trouble. Warts could grow in the most conspicuous places. Momma Opalona's warts, even more so. Not only on your nose, as you would expect. But on the skin of both eyelids, so when you blinked your eyes, the whole world would know that Momma Opalona had it in for you.

Of course, my momma said that was all a lie, too. Same as calling the old woman a witch. Didn't matter to most kids what our mommas said. Among ourselves, only the bravest would actually go down and knock on the woman's door. The ones who did boasted about it like it was something dangerous. Hannah Jane always did ponder dangerous things.

"Please go with me, Chess," she said. "I'm a-scared to go by myself."

She lied. Didn't matter. Not to me. Hannah Jane only had to turn her head to the side, blink her green eyes a time or two, and, oh, that smile. She knew Chester Cumberland would do most near anything she wanted him to do.

"I never been there before," I said. "Wouldn't know where to find her." I said it with my fingers crossed behind my back.

Didn't work. Hannah Jane saw right through me. Everyone knew exactly where to find Momma Opalona's shack. Most kids snuck down there for a peek, one time or another. For sure, they kept their distance, but they waited around just to see if they could catch a glimpse of the old storyteller.

I never did. But it looked like I would now.

"Just knock on the door," Hannah Jane said.

"Maybe she's not home." I prayed the old woman wasn't in.

"Chester, you are such a sissy!" She spoke in her native North Carolina drawl, drawing out the S's on *sissy* so the word sounded much longer than it was. Then she straightened her shoulders and announced, "I'll do it myself, thank you."

She did, too, pushing me out of the way.

The whole shack seemed to shake when she rapped on the door. We waited. It felt forever. No one answered. I couldn't hear anyone rustling around inside—which I would have expected to, because the door was only a few planks of weathered pine bolted to the frame by rusty gate hinges.

"Let's go," I said. "She ain't home, like I told you."

Hannah Jane put her hands on the sides of the red-and-white gingham dress she was so proud of because her momma had made it for her ninth birthday. "Just you wait," she said. She meant it.

While we waited, I got a good look at the holler and Momma Opalona's old pine-plank shack. We had hiked down a draw, about fifty yards off the county road that wound its way in and out of the woods on its way to Robert E. Lee Grade School. With the mountain laurel, rhododendron, and all, the path to her place seemed no wider than it took to pass a body through.

For a stranger to Appalachia, trailing down that cove would be akin to entering another world. Black oak trees, thirty feet around at eye level, towered next to hundred-and-fifty-feet-tall birch and sweet gum trees. I reached down and snatched up a sweet gum ball, just right for tossing at the white squirrels seen only in this part of North Carolina. The chestnuts and hickories and northern red oaks stood together so dense that in the summer, Momma Opalona's shack would never see direct sunlight. Wet and alive it smelled, the scent of new growth in competition with the smell of decay.

We had come a-visiting in the fall. The leaves, almost on fire with red, orange, and yellow, distracted me some from my apprehension. So it didn't seem quite so dark down there just then. But it was dark enough that I stayed scared.

The old shack was just that: old and a shack. The lines in the weathered grain ran deep enough for black widow spiders to set up permanent residences, their little, white, fuzzy nests inviting careless bugs in for a meal. The place leaned to the side just enough for me to wonder how long it would be till it fell over, taking Momma Opalona with it.

I had waited long enough. "Let's go, Hannah Jane. I told you, she ain't home."

Hannah Jane sighed and looked at me like she hadn't decided what to do yet. "Okay," she said, "but I'm a-coming back tomorrow."

We turned to leave and were just about to hike back up the old path, when the door opened behind us. First, I heard the hinges creak, then the voice, scratchy and commanding, calling out to us: "You children's mommas know you here?"

"Yes, ma'am," we lied together without turning around.

"Well, come on in, then," she said. Momma Opalona wasn't asking. She was telling.

By the time we turned around, she had, also. All I could see was the back of a tattered and faded gray homespun dress. The woman bowed over, so I couldn't see the top of her head. A black hand, wrinkled and skinny as a skeleton, wrapped around a slender, knotty oak walking stick that looked taller than the woman herself.

She shuffled her feet into the dark room to a large bird's-eye maple bed. The headboard stood easily five feet tall, with carved scroll designs and big knobs on the posts that looked so intricate, someone must have spent a summer or so whittling. The legs of the bed, where I could see, ended in a claw and ball.

Hannah Jane and I took another step or two into the shack. Across the room from the bed, an iron, coal cookstove radiated enough heat to keep the room warm against the autumn afternoon. A blue porcelain kettle simmered with coffee that smelled as inviting as the sweet, fresh bread cooling on top of the stove. My mouth watered in spite of the lump in my throat. Next to the bed, a large mahogany chifforobe leaned against the wall that itself leaned off-center like it would someday let go of the ceiling and roof, killing all the occupants within.

My luck, it will be today, I thought.

By now, Momma Opalona had reached her bed. She turned and sunk down into the quilt. "Sit down," she said, pointing to a three-foot pine bench, placed parallel to the side of her bed. Between the bed and the bench stood a short table sawn from the cross-section of a hickory tree. It appeared about four inches thick, a couple of feet across, and it rested on four hickory branches cut to fit like dowels into holes cored into the slab. The table centered on a braided rag rug, woven together from pieces of throwaway.

Momma Opalona smiled. I think. I wasn't sure, because I was distracted by her teeth. All three of them. Two on top with a gap big as mine, and one on the bottom. That's all she had in her mouth: three teeth, long and yellow-brown, sticking out like stiff corn stubble.

"That there's the listening place," she said, pointing at the bench with a long finger of the hand she used to hold onto her walking stick. "This," she said, tapping the stick on the plank floor under her feet, "this here's the telling place. You sit there, you listen! I sit here, I tell. You gets old as me, you can tell, too. You not old as Momma Opalona, is you, honey?" She looked straight at Hannah Jane.

"No, ma'am." Hannah Jane was as tongue-tied as me. We both got the message: Whoever comes into Momma Opalona's shack comes to listen—and speaks only when asked to.

"Gooood," Momma Opalona said. "You never wanna be this old, honey. Why don't you go on over that stove yonder. Cut you two slices of that warm bread, one for you'self, other for you boyfriend."

I swear I saw Hannah Jane's face turn red, but I didn't have time to enjoy it, because the next words out of Momma Opalona's mouth were meant for me:

"And you, young sir, you go on over there"—she pointed to a white oak icebox across the room from the stove—"and fetch two strawberry soda waters."

While we prepared our pre-story snack, Momma Opalona nestled into the bed, settling into the feather mattress like a black bird nesting for the evening. She fixed her eyes ahead, not looking to see how we fared. If she noticed me staring at her, she didn't seem to mind. I had never seen a woman so ancient.

Her body looked as skeleton skinny as her hands. The lines in her black face appeared white with age and made me think of the leather seats in my aunt's Model T Ford. I blinked, and her eyes now focused on us with an intensity that made me wonder if she couldn't look right through us. Large eyes, big around, the whites no longer white, but a kind of sad yellow. Yellow, like the newspapers she used on the walls of her shack to keep the wind and cold out. Her feet had grown big for her body. Or maybe just seemed so for all the socks she wore and the wool house slippers with the picture of an Indian chief woven into the fabric.

But it was the irises of her eyes that mostly kept my attention. They weren't brown like the other colored folk I knew. They had lost their color, faded to a kind of hazel, almost green. And they smiled. If I live to be a hundred—which I suspect Momma Opalona had already seen—I don't think I'll ever forget those eyes that smiled.

"I know why y'all come," she said.

Hannah Jane and I looked at each other, both munching on the buttery, sweet bread that would have kept us quiet even if Momma Opalona hadn't laid down the law.

"Y'all wants hear abouts the mystery of Devil's Mountain," she said.

I swallowed hard. Out of the corner of my eyes, I saw Hannah Jane do the same.

Then the old storyteller cackled. She threw back her head and cackled so loud and long and ominously that I wondered no more. My momma was mistaken. Hannah Jane was right. It could be no other way.

That's when I knew for sure.

Momma Opalona really was a witch.

CHAPTER THREE

From high in space the earth they found,
And dumped their garbage on our ground.

MOMMA OPALONA tapped her knotty oak stick three times on the floor. It sounded hollow, like the thump of a finger against the sound-board of a flat-top guitar. Some kids said her stick could turn into a snake, like the staff of Moses. Others said it was really the handle of her broom—and you know what witches can do with a broom. But Momma Opalona said different.

"This be my story staff. Tap times three, story time be. Tap times four, out the door." Her eyes met mine and then Hannah Jane's. "Best be awake for both." We stayed awake.

Momma Opalona, on the other hand, didn't.

She lost her smile. She put her head down against her chest, so it seemed to hide between her knobby shoulders. She closed her eyes. I wasn't sure if she was praying or sleeping. Just when I had decided she was sleeping, she raised her head, looked me in the eyes, and started the story:

"Devil's Mountain be inhabited by folks from another planet, from outer space."

Hannah Jane and I kept our heads straight ahead, but our eyes peeked over at each other. Momma Opalona's hand, the one that wasn't holding the staff, shot out suddenly in front of her body to catch our attention, which wasn't necessary.

"Aliens," she whispered. "Vampire aliens."

I felt a shiver start down the back of my neck and work itself through my body till my toes tingled.

Momma Opalona smiled. "This be how they came to be. Weren't because this county be called Transylvania. You don't be believing all them stories 'bout vampires coming over on sailing ships and such. Ain't no such relationship at all. No sir, not at all. No such thing. Not a'tall. This-here county be called Transylvania 'cause that be Latin for 'across the forest.' No finer forest in the world; no sir. So that be the reason for the name Transylvania." She paused for effect before she said, "Which don't mean they ain't no vampires out here'bouts." She cackled again.

Hannah Jane and I did our eye-contact thing again. I'm sure she wondered, as I did, if Momma Opalona had just made that up. We didn't worry about it for long. The old woman finished her history lesson and got straight to the story:

"They be abandoned up yonder, them alien folks, like so much garbage." She pointed in the direction of Devil's Mountain, which sat close enough to town for us to look at it every day and wonder.

"They be abandoned up there by they very own people. They be rebels, not wanted on they very own planet. So one winter, just after the War Between the States—our time, that is—they be taken in they spaceships and dumped off like so much garbage, right up yonder on top that mountain." She pointed again in the direction of Devil's Mountain.

"I suppose you young'ns wants to hear how come Momma Opalona comes to know all this?"

We didn't answer. Our mouths had even stopped chewing on the bread. We nodded together, a fraction of an inch or so, but it was enough for Momma Opalona.

"My very own momma told me, that be why-because," she said. "Momma knowed 'cause she be the only woman who seen them aliens and lives to tell 'bout it. Not that the others be dead, the other ones who seen them and never come back down that mountain. They ain't dead. Course, they ain't exactly alive, neither."

She stood up from her bed and shuffled over to the footboard, where a tapestry partially covered a wooden steamer trunk adorned with tarnished brass braces and hardware. She tapped the trunk with her stick. "One these days, old Momma Opalona show y'all the contents of this-here trunk. Y'all be surprised."

This is just a story, I thought to myself, at the same time as I promised never ever to go anywhere near Devil's Mountain—just in case.

The old storyteller walked from the trunk over to where we sat. She stood right in front of us. I could feel her eyes go right through me. "You be thinking, this just be a made-up story," she said, looking straight into my eyes. "That kind of thinking be what got the others in trouble. And you"—her long finger pointed at Hannah

Jane—"you believes me, but you gots a notion to see for you'self all the same. Don't matter what I says to the contrary." Momma Opalona knew Hannah Jane without once having had a conversation with her.

"Stay away, young'ns. Listen to old Momma Opalona, now. Stay away from that evil mountain."

I will, Momma Opalona, I thought, knowing she could hear every word that rolled around in my head. *I cross my heart and hope to die. I never will set foot on that mountain.*

I could hear that promise for years. Same as I heard it that eventful night when the moon arrived full, during the autumn of my last year in high school. I stood at the back of Brevard High. I stood there with John Croshaw, the boy I hated. Together, the two of us—waiting for Hannah Jane Goins, so we could start our hike up Devil's Mountain. I promised Momma Opalona I would never ascend that evil place. I wished Hannah Jane and I had kept that promise.

CHAPTER FOUR

Ahooooo! I hear when night is near
And wind blows through the trees,
The kind of sounds that makes hearts pound
And brings me to my knees.

JOHN CROSHAW kicked the dirt and talked to himself, ignoring me best he could. Almost dark now. We had been waiting ten minutes for Hannah Jane. If he expected her to be on time, I had news for him. Hannah Jane never arrived on time. I'd learned to wait. His turn now.

He looked like he knew how to dress for a long hike. The weather wasn't all that cold, though the trees had started to turn their fall colors, and patches of an early snow dotted the mountainside. John Croshaw wore khaki trousers and leather hiking boots. My tennis shoes looked cheap in comparison. Of course, they *were* cheap. He had on a green lined jacket—pockets everywhere—over a brown wool shirt. A wool cap stood on top of his head. All his clothes looked new to me. Very much like the fancy clothes you could buy from the town's only authentic department store. The one that had been burglarized just before school started. I had wondered about that. I discounted my suspicions as the product of a jealous heart. Still, it did seem strange that everything John Croshaw wore seemed as new as Christmas shirts.

I, on the other hand, wore my old watch cap and a mackinaw jacket my daddy had handed down to me when I got big enough to wear it with the sleeves rolled up a couple times. My jeans came compliments of one of my uncles who had gone off to fight in Korea. I remember thinking how grown-up I must have looked in them. They were not new, but they fit better than my jacket.

John Croshaw kicked the dirt and gravel again and again, then he looked at his watch and sighed loud enough to let me know he was getting more irritated. I noticed that the time seemed so important to him. A perfectionist, I decided. Though, I do recall wondering if there was something else. I discounted that. I felt as if I could share his consternation over Hannah Jane's tardiness, but I still didn't like him. The more I knew about him, the less I liked.

I suppose, looking back, it was because there wasn't much to know about John Croshaw. He told anyone who asked that he came from another state. When asked which state, he said it wasn't important. No one had ever met his parents. I surmised that they had to be too important to want to associate with the likes of us. The house where he lived lay down a county road. A "No Trespassing" sign interrupted any plans to satisfy curiosity.

I made up my mind that night that I would be civil to John Croshaw because Hannah Jane loved him. I tried. A waste of time. He acted no happier with me being there than he was with Hannah Jane being her usual late self.

"Want an RC?" I offered, pulling two of the giant-sized cola bottles from the knapsack I had brought along for the hike. I held one up for his appraisal.

"Give it to me." No hesitation. No thank-you. He jerked the bottle from my hand, then it must have come to him that I had something he needed. He held his hand out with a "Well?"

I offered him the church key. He snapped the cap like he couldn't wait to get into the contents. If even then he said thank you, I didn't hear it. A fourth of the way through the process of trying to guzzle down the bottle in one long swallow, John Croshaw was ill prepared for the arrival of Hannah Jane, who made her "surprise" appearance from behind a mountain laurel bush.

"Johnny, Johnny, Johnny Croshaw," she whispered in his ear, a fraction of an inch from his Royal-Crown-Cola-swallowing face. She caught him by surprise, all right.

"Whaaa—!" He got half a *what* out before he choked on the drink, sending soda pop and carbonated snot foaming out his mouth and nose. I had never seen John Croshaw look *finer*.

Hannah Jane didn't know whether to laugh, get out of the way, or try to help. John Croshaw's face showed anger, but every time he tried to tell us about it, he choked again. I almost started to believe that the night would be worthwhile. Then a rumble of thunder and a cold wind howling down the mountain told me I was wrong.

I was right: I was wrong.

* * *

Our climb started out easy enough. Like her new heartthrob, Hannah Jane also knew how to dress for a hike, but she didn't. She hadn't dressed for the weather; she'd dressed for Johnny. I was sure of it. Her pedal pushers and tennis shoes looked fresh off the rack. The pink sweater she wore clung too tightly to her body to ward off the wind. She had combed her hair and puffed it up in the front like she was going to church.

If she froze to death, I reckoned, that would have been okay with me. Then I thought, *Johnny will probably keep her warm.*

He hiked up the trail like some kind of long-distance runner. Hannah Jane kept up fine. I did too, for a mile or so. Then I felt like throwing up.

"Wait up," I called to them. They had outpaced me by about twenty yards.

"You okay, Chess?" Hannah Jane called back.

"If he can't keep up, he'll have to go home." John Croshaw spoke to Hannah Jane, careful not to look at me.

"I'm fine," I lied. I would keep up. I would rather puke every step to the top of Devil's Mountain before I let that boy be alone with Hannah Jane. Somewhere in the back of my mind, though, I worried that I might not be able to keep up. Worse, I tried not to surmise that Hannah Jane might not want me to keep up, either.

Three miles up a trail that rose steadily through old-growth forest, we reached a chain-link fence with a sign that said:
GOVERNMENT RESERVATION
RESTRICTED AREA
VIOLATORS WILL BE PROSECUTED

I was about to say *We gotta go back*, when John Croshaw laughed and said, "We're not going to let some old Army posted sign stop us, are we?"

"What do you mean, *we*?" I said.

He looked at me like my daddy did when he caught me doing something childish. "You're not scared, are you, Chester?" It was the first time he referred to me by my name, and it was to insult me.

"I'm not scared. I just don't believe in breaking the law."

He laughed. "This," he said, pointing to the sign, "is a joke."

"Maybe to you—" I began.

He cut me off. "My father is in Army Intelligence. That's why you never see him. This property was used for maneuvers way back in World War II. Why do you think I'm not afraid of vampires?" He said the word like a bigger kid would say *Santa Claus* to a little child. "I know there's nothing up here to be afraid of, unless you're afraid of kids' stories." He looked straight at me with eyes blue as a calm mountain lake.

Anything I would have said about Momma Opalona would have been ridiculed. To be honest, I was beginning to wonder myself.

"Let's go," I said, trying to look like I had never been afraid of anything in my life. Inside, my stomach felt full of bugs.

John Croshaw climbed the fence with ease. Barbed wire strung across the top had long ago rusted through. He straddled the top and reached down to Hannah Jane.

"Thank you, Johnny." Had it been me offering her help, she would have said, "Thank you, but I can do it myself."

I struggled over, making little grunting sounds as I tugged to free my knapsack from a stray piece of barbed wire. I watched John Croshaw grin back at me as he and Hannah Jane took off up the trail.

You did it again, I said to myself. *Let someone talk you into doing something stupid.* That didn't stop me from following.

The trail wound lazily, for a time, through rhododendron bushes, ground fern, and white trillium, and over fallen pine and hard-wood stumps. Perfect black-bear country. I tried not to think of that. No one I'd known had ever gone up here—not during the day, not at night, and never on a full moon. Not anyone who ever listened to Momma Opalona. I could hear her cackling.

"Never on a full moon," she'd said. "Worst time ever. Full moon gives them greater power. You gonna be a fool, go up daytime. Night, if you crazy. But, you wants never to come back, go on up there on a full moon." I saw her eyes, those smiling eyes, but they hadn't been smiling just then. Momma Opalona was serious. Dead serious. "Never on a full moon."

Tonight was a hunter's moon, about as full as the moon gets.

John Croshaw talked to Hannah Jane. I listened from my position several yards behind. "We're following Deadline Creek," he said. "Follows the lay of the mountain."

How did he know that? A tinge of fear ran down my spine. How did he know that?

He continued, "Once we cross the creek, we're in enemy territory."

"Sure," Hannah Jane said, then she laughed.

Isn't he clever. I couldn't get it out of my system. He spoke of the mountain as if it were an old friend. A stranger to these parts? From another state? The pit of my stomach turned over a few times more.

"You're not doing bad." He touched her on the arm when he spoke. I was sure he raised his voice a little to make sure I heard him.

Hannah Jane said, "My mommy and daddy took me on my first hike in a knapsack. I've been doing this all my life." She looked at him the way I had wanted her to look at me.

Too late, Chess, I told myself. *It's all over but the church wedding.* In my imagination, the whole affair took form. The wedding. Hannah Jane, happier than I could ever make her. Johnny, all smiles, his daddy smiling in his Army uniform with five stars on his shoulder, not to mention his own momma. A picture-show movie star, what else?

"How old are you?" he asked Hannah Jane.

Oh, my goodness, it was true. John Croshaw was about to ask her to marry him and have children.

"Eighteen," she lied. I knew she would. My stomach started hurting so bad, I thought I would pass out from the pain. I decided the only thing that kept me going was the sight of John Croshaw's perfect teeth grinning down at me all the while he talked to Hannah Jane.

"I just thought of something," he said.

Hannah Jane smiled. "Yes, Johnny?"

"Did you tell anyone we were coming up here?"

She hesitated. "Honest?" she said.

"Honest, Hannah Jane, did you?"

She got her cute look on her face. Then she cocked her head like she always did when she wanted out of trouble. "My parents don't know," she said. "I snuck out. But I made a real big mistake, I suppose."

"What mistake?" His face darkened a shade.

"I got so excited about coming up here . . . with you . . . that I let it slip to my little sister, Martha Anne, that little blabbermouth. Well, I suppose it had to come out, anyway. I think I'm in big trouble when I get home. Bad enough I sneak out at night. But to be with a boy. . . ." She didn't even say *boys*, like I already didn't exist to her. Not enough that John Croshaw ignored me. Now Hannah Jane added the insult.

He reached over and put his arm around her and gave her a little hug. "Don't worry," he said to her, "I'll tell them it was all my idea. Besides, I won't even touch you."

You already have, you rat! I pictured myself a foot taller, standing over him saying, *You already have, you rat!*

Hannah Jane touched her shoulder where he had hugged her. That didn't help my stomach any.

It had been impossible to see the moon clearly for the trees until we dropped into a clearing of smooth rock about thirty feet across. "Whoooa," I heard Hannah Jane say. "It really is eerie out here like this. I can see how little kids would believe a story about aliens."

"Vampire aliens," John Croshaw said. Then he bent over like Bela Lugosi and pretended he was going to bite her on the neck. "Huh-huh-huh-huh-huh-huh, I veeelll make you my bride." He slobbered all over her neck, and all Hannah Jane did was giggle.

I had to find a way to keep from making a fool out of myself by challenging him to a fight I could never win. So I forced myself to study the terrain. It really was eerie.

From where we had climbed, the mountain looked different from how it looked at the bottom of the trail. The moonlight revealed deep cuts and gorges etched into the landscape. No peak like most mountains. Instead, a sharply cut rocky ridge rode parallel to the horizon, across the crest.

"That must be Devil's Head," Hannah Jane said. She meant the very top of Devil's Mountain, which folks called Devil's Head.

Beware Devil's Head, I heard Momma Opalona say. *Once a body crosses into Devil's Head, it be too late to turn back.* She hadn't smiled when she said it, neither. I could see her, clear as day, the old storyteller:

She shook her head back and forth, looking first at Hannah Jane, then at me. "You children know the story of Devil's Head, don't you?"

She knew we didn't, not the official Momma Opalona version, which, in our day, was the only official version.

"Devil's Head be the very place they make childrens into vampires. On the full moon, when them aliens' power be the greatest, they takes they captive young'ns and makes them into vampires, like theyselves."

John Croshaw's voice interrupted my memory. "Looks like it's going to be a harder climb than I thought." He looked directly down at me. "You can go back now, Chester." He wasn't asking; he was telling me.

The way he said it sort of pushed a button inside my mind that told me I was about to be in for that beating I so feared. The voice said, *Chester Cumberland, you may get whipped, but you ain't about to be humiliated.*

I got my back up and said to him, "I'll go when I'm good and ready, sir," sounding firm like my daddy did when he got his own back up.

I guess John Croshaw got the message, because he just laughed and said, "Suit yourself," then started climbing. He made sure he took ahold of Hannah Jane's hand as he did. I had to give it to him. There are ways to hurt a body better than a beating.

We were just about to drop into a long dark gully, when he stopped and looked back down the mountain.

"What?" Hannah Jane's voice had a touch of uncertainty to it. She leaned forward, trying to get a better take on the darkness in front of her.

I looked too. Saw nothing but black.

John Croshaw stared for a while longer. "Nothing," he said. "Clouds sure cast weird shadows, don't they?"

We continued along the gulch. Clouds covered the moon again. It became almost pitch black. Wind whistled through the cut like in the Abbott and Costello horror picture shows I had seen down at the Rialto. You could almost hear Lon Chaney Jr. howling at the moon, while Bela Lugosi turned into a bat and took after his fleeing victim.

My pace picked up. I didn't have any trouble staying close to them in that dark place. I had to. Moss covered the walls of the cracks in the mountainside. I smelled mold and decaying wood, and felt along the sides, hoping I wouldn't touch something that moved.

"I'm cold," Hannah Jane complained.

Serves you right, I thought. *Next time you'll dress for the weather, not to please Mr. Perfect.*

"It'll be okay," he said. "Stay closer to me."

I knew it.

He stopped, and I ran into Hannah Jane, the closest to her I had ever been—and it was an accident.

"Shhhhh," he said. "I heard something."

We waited. Nothing. Except for the wind, there was no sound at all. Then, faintly, I heard it too.

"I hear it, too," Hannah Jane said.

It was distant at first, gradually growing louder, like there was something climbing up the mountain behind us. We all kept our places, listening, trying to figure out what it was that seemed to be following us up that ugly mountain. After a while, there was no doubt: Whatever was down there was headed in our direction.

John Croshaw whispered, "They're down the gap behind us."

I heard it again. Breathing. For a-certain, I could hear breathing. That's when I realized there were several of them. I wanted to ask, *Do vampires breathe?* They seemed to be on the sides of us now. The rustling of bodies. Breathing bodies. Footsteps. Footsteps closer now. I was so scared, I thought my heart would jump right out of my mouth.

Then John Croshaw said the first words I agreed with all night: "I don't like the sound of this. They're all around us now, everywhere except straight up."

"Animals?" Hannah Jane asked.

He answered, "Not the kind we'd like to meet, I imagine. Listen!"

Breathing heavier now. Gasping for air. Almost on top of us.

No one had to say it. We ran for it. We took off straight uphill. For the first time since we started, I had no trouble keeping up. Whoever they were, they were behind and on both sides of us. There was no place to go. No place except to where it seemed we were being herded, straight toward Devil's Head.

Times like this, times when I experience fear of the unknown, I would tell myself not to worry. At least, not to invent monsters that didn't exist. Like a picture show, the events that sometimes came to haunt me could be resolved when I told myself, *It's just like a picture show.* A part of my imagination simply got out of control. Oh, how I wished that would have been true.

CHAPTER FIVE

Flying saucers fly at night,
Martians manned and armed for fright.
Learn this lesson, learn it right:
Never, never roam at night.
Keep to home when full moons show.
Dark roads beckon fools to go
Down the places spaceships glow.
Learn this lesson where to go:
Never down the dark ways, no.
Learn this lesson where to go,
Lesson from the picture show.

EVERYONE KNEW that alien creatures from outer space had long ago invaded our planet. In 1947 a space ship crashed in Roswell, New Mexico. Yes, the authorities tried to cover it all up. But we knew better. After all, we had the picture shows.

My daddy thought otherwise. He insisted it was all made up. Like the professional wrestler, Gorgeous George, who wore bobby pins and dyed his curly hair platinum and threw kisses to the audience. All a show. "Not real," said Daddy. A part of me wanted to believe him. Especially when I was afraid at night.

My daddy had to remind me, "There ain't no such a thing as monsters."

I had to remind myself of that when the moon shadows were just right in the bedroom I shared with my brother, Aldous. My junior by less than a year, with curly hair and no cowlick, Aldous slept with me in the same squeaky iron bed all the way till I left home after high school. Smarter than me, Aldous figured out that if he fell asleep before me, he didn't have to fret over the creatures that crept out of closets and from under beds at night.

So there I would lie, wide awake, listening to the creaks in dark corners and watching for strange shadows that inevitably presented themselves after a daytime adventure with dangerous consequences. Like the time Daddy took the two of us to a traveling carnival, which featured real live alligators and crocodiles. The alligator man—as he referred to himself—had a thumb missing on his right hand. Aldous whispered, "Betcha he loses the other one today."

The man stood inside a makeshift pit, just high enough for a kid to see over if he stood on his tiptoes. No one had to tell us the purpose of the pit. But just in case, the alligator man made it all perfectly clear: "For y'all's protection," he said.

A short, wiry man, he never stopped talking, sharing secrets about the reptilian world that none of us ever knew. While he talked, he walked. I marveled at how calmly he strolled among the hissing and snapping creatures until he selected one for special attention. Special attention, meaning he would wrestle the creature, which did not suffer the activity without a fight.

Aldous had been quick to hide his face in his hands during the struggle, which gave me my chance to put one over on him. I nudged him and said, "Hey, look at the blood. You was right, Aldous—thumb, hand, all the way up to the elbow. Chop, chop, chop, gulp. Ain't you gonna look?"

That night, I got my comeuppance when the dog licked my hand, while it hung over the side of the bed, in the middle of a vivid dream about being chased by alligators.

A fright? You bet. But that was nothing compared to the moving picture show I attended for the first and only time in the company of Hannah Jane.

We were just short of seventeen, and for some unknown reason, she accepted my offer to pay her way to the show. I tried to hide my excitement from the family, but Aldous did his best to point out how my cowlick was suddenly under control and that I did smell good enough to be plucked and put in a vase.

My expectations of the moment came with a price.

"Aw, Mom."

She stood her ground, my mother's brown eyes the picture of uncompromising authority. "Aldous goes with you, or no one goes."

My mother knew nothing of love. "Aw, Mom, he goes everywhere with me. How about just this once?"

My begging and pleading with Momma changed nothing. She reached for daddy's razor strop near the kitchen sink—a largely symbolic gesture then, since I stood a full head taller than her. But, she was my mom.

I conceded defeat. "Okay, I'll take him." In my mind I had to make a quick adjustment. Aldous could go with us. But he would have to sit by himself.

It would be his first time alone at the Rialto. A part of me felt sorry for him. Though not enough for me to allow him to sit with Hannah Jane and me.

The old theater held its moments for my brother and me. There were the 9¢ Saturday matinee serials. When we were seven or so, our perspectives magnified life. The marquee looked like something out of some big city, neon lights flashing and the name of the picture show and stars standing out so bold a boy could just drool to get inside and encounter the magic. At first, though, you had to pass through the scent of urine, forever embedded in the rich carpets from when the toilets overflowed. By the time the smell of buttered popcorn took over, all was forgiven.

I couldn't have imagined a more appropriate place to impress Hannah Jane on our first date. She did not seem to share my enthusiasm.

Hannah Jane said nothing about my appearance nor even about my brother trailing behind us as I had instructed, nor did she seem in awe of the Rialto's trappings. Her interest focused on the movie alone, a horror film called *Invasion of the Body Snatchers*.

We got preliminaries over in a hurry. Aldous found a place in the middle of the theater. I followed Hannah Jane, who marched all the way to the front row.

She insisted, "I want my money's worth. This is gonna be real scary, and I want to be up close so I can get the full effect. I do so expect to get scared from here to Asheville."

My own expectations wavered in a different direction.

"Chester. What are you doing with that arm of yours?"

I froze in midair, my hand just about to close down on Hannah Jane's shoulder. I had managed to sneak my arm close enough to feel the heat of it. As near as I would get that evening. "Just trying to scratch the back of my neck, right back here where it itches."

"Chester, that ain't your neck you're aiming to scratch. Now, you just go on and put your hand back where it belongs."

The blessing of movie theaters is that you can't see a body blush.

If I felt disappointed, I found solace in the movie. Indeed, by the time the good guy managed to avoid the alien pods that duplicated the bodies of every earthling in his small town, my mind no longer strayed toward Hannah Jane.

That night, I forced myself to stay awake, knowing that you could only be replaced by an alien pod if you fall asleep. Every branch brushing against the side of the house, every rustle in the bushes, every insect scratching its wings, every gust of wind alerted me to the possibility of alien invasion. Even the glow of the fireflies caused me a fright. This time, I had company. Aldous kept watch with me.

"You don't suppose there really are alien pods and such," he offered.

I lied to reassure both of us. "No such thing, Aldous. Truth is, I just don't feel sleepy tonight."

"Me, neither." He yawned. "You will nudge me in case I start to fall off to sleep, won't you?"

I'm not sure I would have made it safely through that night without him. By the second evening, I had pretty much lost my fear of aliens and collapsed into a deep sleep out of sheer exhaustion. Aldous had crashed hours before me. I had to push him over to make room for me in the bed.

Monday morning, I awoke to a lump next to me in bed. Not my brother. Something had taken up residence right in the middle of the two of us. I peeked under the covers only long enough to confirm my fears. By the time I reached the back door, my heart thumped loud enough, I swear I heard it beating out its message of pure horror.

I wanted to scream, but the humiliation of it kept my mouth shut. That's when it struck me. I had left my brother alone in bed by himself with. . . . And that's the precise time I heard the scream.

Aldous had no reticence about letting his real feelings be known. He screamed so, the dogs barked and the rooster crowed. He screamed on his way out of the bedroom and on his way past me through the back door and into the yard, where my daddy, who had been out there puttering, got ahold of him.

Then Momma ran by me out into the yard, muttering something like "I don't know what you did to your brother, Chester, but you better fess up by the time I come back to get my hands on you."

Thankfully, school started too early for anyone to assign blame. Between classes, Hannah Jane went out of her way to find me and ask how I liked the picture show, and added, "By the way, Chester, you ain't mad at me or nothing."

"Mad at what?"

"Oh, nothing a body should be a-scared of." She smiled and sashayed off, while my brain started the process of putting it all together.

Someone familiar enough with our family to know that Aldous and I slept, in the summer, with an open window had managed to slip into our bedroom the night before. And while we slept soundly for the first time in two days, that someone inserted a two-foot-long zucchini squash in our bed right between the two of us.

A dirty trick if there ever was one.

Now, on Devil's Mountain, I found myself wanting it all to be a trick Hannah Jane had played on me, just one more time. But if it was only pretend, I was certain the trick was not over yet. For, unless my senses had deceived me, there was plenty to be a-scared about just now. Oh, how I did pray it would all be a trick.

CHAPTER SIX

And all around I hear the sound
Of searchers in the wood,
Who search the snow, I do not know,
For evil or for good.

TRICK OR NO TRICK, we moved as fast as we could through the darkness. Whoever shadowed us kept close, like they knew the direction we had chosen. I stumbled in a small snow drift and fell, then pulled myself to my feet, brushing the snow from my clothes. That's when it hit me. "Hey," I whispered, "it's the snow. They're following our footsteps in the snow."

No one took the time to respond to me.

Soon, I heard the sound of voices. Guttural, almost grunting, like they were as out of breath, struggling against nature, as we were. The cut through which we ran acted as an echo chamber.

John Croshaw whispered, "Be quiet."

We stopped and listened. They were close enough that I heard them talking.

"They're up ahead somewhere," one of them said. This voice low, in control. The speaker sounded as if he were giving orders. But who?

My mind ached. Confused. How could alien vampires speak our language? Maybe they're soldiers? Our own soldiers. After all, we were trespassing on government property. Then, maybe, they're soldiers of another kind?

Another one spoke, his voice higher. He seemed to have the same raspiness as the first one. "Yes, I think you're right. They seem to be just up there. I heard them run, but not now. Maybe they just stopped."

Our pursuers had stopped too, doing the same as us, listening, trying to get a fix on our location.

The first one spoke again. "Is your weapon loaded?"

I heard Hannah Jane take a deep breath. I could imagine it all, ray guns or whatever, preparing to zap us if we resisted. I stopped thinking when the other man answered:

"What did you say?"

"Your weapon! Is it loaded? Are you prepared to use it?"

"Yeah, it's ready. So am I."

That was all we needed to hear. We took off again, a straight line up the mountain.

They heard us. One of them screamed, "Hey, stop!"

We didn't stop.

Our pursuers picked up their pace.

A foot race now. Us against. . . .

"I don't like the odds," John Croshaw said. "They know what they're doing, staying in a half circle, herding us like animals."

The clouds had partially exposed the moon. We could see our trail better. The trees clumped much thicker now. Less snow covered the ground.

"Can you see them?" John Croshaw said, speaking for the first time without sounding like he was talking down to me.

"No," I said. My breath came in spurts I tried hard to control. "But whoever they are, they don't sound very friendly."

Hannah Jane made a little *ooooh* noise, then asked John Croshaw, "What do we do now?" He didn't answer, so she said what I had been afraid to admit: "This ain't a joke no more. Those people are trying to kill us!"

John Croshaw said, "We got to hide somewhere. They're gaining on us, running us till we get tired, like hunting animals. They know what they're doing. We gotta find a place to hide."

We kept climbing, looking for something—a log, a deep culvert, maybe a dense clump of brush or ferns—to lie in and hide. John Croshaw had it figured right. We couldn't outrun them. Our only hope, a place to hide and pray they wouldn't find us. Maybe they would just pass us by and we could go on home. Maybe. . . .

He stopped. "There!" He pointed to an eroded opening in the bank of a dry creek bed. A five-foot wash, cut by centuries of rain, contained the tiny cave. Because the cave lay alee of the wind, the snow drifted to the other side of the cut. We could walk there without leaving tracks. "It's not much," he admitted, "but I think we can squeeze in."

We found some brush and broken branches from a rhododendron bush to stack in front of the opening. John Croshaw and I pulled the branches in front of us as we scooted backwards inside the small cave. There wasn't room to stand or even sit. We had to lie there on our stomachs, hoping like crazy the plan would work. We waited. It was quiet, deadly quiet. Not even the wind whipped through the cut.

I felt Hannah Jane shivering between us. That's when the irony of our situation struck me. I had never in my entire life been so close to the object of my undying affection. I could feel her body trembling next to mine. I discovered I had this sudden, deep urge to protect her. I allowed that my intentions toward her were honest, and caring, and chivalrous. Momma always said chivalry from the Southern gentleman is dead. That cold night, I would prove my momma wrong again.

Looking back, the craziness of it comes out full force. But back then, in the heat of a chase, it came to me that Hannah Jane would not resist were I to reach my arm over to touch her protectively. So, I did it. I lifted my arm and laid it gently on top of . . . John Croshaw's arm.

He beat me to it again. Those little bugs in my stomach started to crawl like crazy.

Her face was turned away from me, looking, I was sure, into blue eyes as calm as a mountain lake. He would be looking into her eyes too. Then it hit me so, I almost forgot we were in the middle of a possible alien attack: *Oh, my goodness, he's going to kiss her . . . and she surely wants him to.* Their lips would be inches apart.

I saw my entire life pass before me. I felt my heart sinking fast. All I could think to do was put my hands against my ears so I couldn't hear the slurp when they did it.

Funny how something as innocent and simple as a kiss could have caused me such consternation just then. Back in those days, though, a kiss was just as near as a boy could get to a girl without actually crossing over the line of custom and morality, by which we measured our relationships. A kiss was not just a kiss, as a classic song of the day would have had us believe. A kiss was a promise, most near a vow of engagement as there was around those times.

Fact is, no one would dare to be seen kissing—or "necking," as we called it—in public. My first kiss, the one and only time I got suckered into a game of spin the bottle, had taken place in a dark closet so no one could see it happen, not even the two of us doing the kissing. I discovered only that I was so bad at kissing, I took the vow then and there to save my future kisses for marriage. For marriage to Hannah Jane Goins. And now, she was in the process of breaking my promise for me by kissing another boy. For me, all was lost.

That's when it happened. A scrape outside the cave. I was saved, though I didn't know it right away.

I felt Hannah Jane's body stiffen. Did his kiss kill her? I looked over. No one was moving. Again, a scrape. Someone stood outside our cave. I tried not to move. When I took my hands from my ears, I heard the voices echoing down the gully, very close to our hiding place.

I recognized the first one who spoke. The one who seemed to be giving orders. He said, "I know I saw them down this cut."

I regretted squeezing into the cave, now a death trap.

Another one spoke, a voice I hadn't heard before. Shrill, agitated, the voice broke often, and the speaker kept clearing his throat. "Are you sure?" he said. "I can't see how anyone could hide down here."

The gravelly voiced one said, "You two get down there and find them. I know they're in that wash. Don't argue with me."

A few moments later, we heard footsteps coming closer. They stopped, directly in front of our hiding place. Too dark to make them out clearly. All three of us sucked in as much air as we could. We held our breath and waited. We couldn't make a sound. I was sure they would be able to hear my heart beating.

One of them spoke, this time in a whisper. "See, like I said, there's no one down here."

The other one let out a little snicker and whispered back, "Maybe they're already dead."

I couldn't help myself. I jerked back into the cave a little more.

"What was that?" one of them said. They stayed still and listened.

I was about to pass out from holding my breath. I felt Hannah Jane press her hands on the ground like she would, too. Just when I thought I couldn't hold it a second more, they started to move on. I wanted to scream. Instead, I pursed my lips like I was playing an oboe and let the air out a little bit at a time. The next breath I took sounded like three breaths because all three of us did it at the same time.

We waited a few more minutes. It had gotten very quiet. They were probably listening for us. All I wanted to do was go home and climb under the covers of my bed and sleep till I was twenty-one.

"We got to go," John Croshaw said.

"I'm all for that," I said. I started to push the bushes from the front of the cave. "I can't wait to get home."

"Me too," Hannah Jane said. "I don't care how much trouble I'm in down there. Nothing could be worse than what's up here."

We had our sights set on home, but John Croshaw had another idea. "We can't get away by going back down that direction." He pointed down the mountain.

"You just watch me," I said.

"Go on, chicken," he said, "get yourself killed, if you want to. Hannah Jane and I are going straight up."

"We are?" Hannah Jane said, disagreeing with him for the first time in their romantic lives.

"Okay, listen," he said. "I wasn't completely honest with you back there."

"I'll say," I added.

"Do you mind," he said. "Look, Chester, I know you and I don't seem to get along. . . ."

Understatement, I thought.

He continued, "But this is life or death, and if you care about Hannah Jane, you'll listen, 'cause it's a matter of getting out of here alive or staying here dead . . . or worse."

I said, "I'm listening."

"Good! Because when I told you my father was in Army Intelligence, I lied."

I wanted to say, *Tell me something I don't already know,* but I let him finish.

"He's not in Intelligence; he's with the Air Force. Father's a scientist. He's here to investigate reports that aliens have invaded the planet and set up an advance colony right here in Transylvania County."

Just like Momma Opalona said.

I wanted to say, *Just like Momma Opalona said,* but after listening to him talk about scientists and such, I knew how stupid it would sound. So instead, I asked, "What's all that have to do with going up there, instead of running down to home?"

"I'm getting to that," he said. "Father has secret reports he keeps in his attic at home. I shouldn't have done it, but I snuck into his office and read the reports. It says that the aliens have hidden entrances all around this mountain. But they're especially concentrated down there." He pointed down to the base of the mountain. "That's why they came at us from the back and sides. Their sensors traced us going past their camouflaged entrances, and they sent their soldiers to follow us up here so they could capture us and. . . ." His voice trailed off, but Hannah Jane and I knew what would come if we were captured.

Hannah Jane spoke. "Okay, Johnny, we believe you."

Speak for yourself, Hannah Jane, I thought. *Love is blind.*

She continued, "But, like Chess said, what has this to do with going up the mountain instead of down?"

"I'm getting to that. In the secret report I read, it said that place up there"—he pointed to Devil's Head—"that place is considered off-limits to the aliens."

"Oh, crap!" I said.

The way he looked at me, there was no mistaking he didn't appreciate my attitude. "Suit yourself," he said, "but Devil's Head is out of bounds for the aliens. The report says so. Says they know they can be spotted by our spy planes if they go up there, and says they can't tolerate too much moonlight."

I said, "Momma Opalona says, moonlight makes them powerful." I regretted it as soon as it came out of my mouth.

He didn't miss a beat. "Oh, she did, did she. Well, of course, we should give her a job with the Air Force. Who needs scientists when we got an old nigger witch sitting down in a holler, telling stupid scaredy-cats all about Martians with vampire teeth."

I wanted to crawl in a hole and die. Instead, I said, "Don't you call her names, hear me?"

He didn't let up. "You go on down there, Chesssster. Maybe Witch Opalona will bail you out. Hannah Jane and I are going up to Devil's Head, where it's safe."

There wasn't anything I could say. I looked at Hannah Jane. She shrugged her shoulders.

John Croshaw crawled out of the cave and offered his hand to her. She looked back at me and rolled her eyes, then took his hand and started up the mountain.

I lay there for a couple of moments, wondering why he always seemed to win. Then I got up and followed. "You're going to regret this," I said to myself.

For once, I was right.

CHAPTER SEVEN

Yes, you'll hear the winds a-howlin'
Like a baby child so dear,
A-wailin' like a baby cries
When evil stalks too near.

I LOOKED AT MY WATCH. Five minutes of midnight. I couldn't believe we had been on the mountain since a little before seven. My stomach grumbled. Not the time to stop for a snack. I still had two bottles of soda and a small army-surplus canteen of water in my knapsack. Extra sandwiches, too.

Because Hannah Jane worried more about impressing John Croshaw than eating, she had carried a small pack that looked like it didn't hold much. John Croshaw had no pack with him, not even a small one. He didn't look like he needed anything to eat, though.

By now, Hannah Jane had fallen back. John Croshaw kept up the same pace he used when we started. We seemed to be getting closer to the ridge, Devil's Head.

The trail widened in parts. I saw more pine trees and less of the hardwoods that prefer lower altitudes. Clouds still played peekaboo with the moon. But mostly, it stayed dark. I was grateful for that. The wind came in gusts, beating against us, sapping our energy. Hannah Jane's and mine, anyway.

It had been some time since we'd heard even a faint sound of the ones who had been following us. I wanted to ask John Croshaw if he knew any more about the aliens who were supposed to inhabit this dreadful mountain, like how it was they came to speak English. But he was so far ahead of both of us, I would have had to yell up at him. So I kept quiet.

Not Hannah Jane. She looked back at me. I was fifteen yards behind her and a good thirty yards from our leader.

"I'm hungry," she said.

"Me too."

"Let's stop. Chess, you got anything in your rucksack?"

She knew I did.

"What about him?" I said.

She looked up the trail and said, "Johnnnnyyy."

He stopped, looked back, then motioned for her to keep up.

She put her hands on her hips and held her ground.

That's my girl, I thought, *not about to miss a meal if she can help it.*

For a few moments, they looked at each other. Then he started down to where she held her ground. When he got there, he had this well-what-now, grown-up look on his face.

"I'm hungry," she said. "Tired too. We need to rest."

"Not yet," he said.

"Yes, now!"

He shook his head and took a deep breath, letting out a sigh I heard from where I rested. "Okay," he said, "but not out here in the open. Up there, where I was"—he pointed with his head—"there's a small outcropping of rocks a little off the trail. We can stop and rest there. Only for a while."

We crashed. Hannah Jane found the soda and a sandwich in my knapsack. John Croshaw sat with his arms around his knees, pulling them close to his chest.

I took a drink of water and lay on my back, looking up at the moon, half covered by clouds. I reached up. It looked so close I thought I could touch it. I wondered if maybe John Croshaw had been right about the aliens preferring to stay lower down the mountain, away from direct moonlight.

I had to admire his endurance. He had gotten us this far. There seemed to be no one following us now. Not a good time to let down my guard. I heard rustling in the underbrush off to my left.

I sat straight up.

"What is it?" Hannah Jane asked.

"Over there," I said, pointing to a thick clump of pine trees and large ground fern.

It rustled again.

Hannah Jane started to stand up, but John Croshaw pulled her to the ground. "Stay low," he said to us. "Don't make a sound."

We sprawled on the ground, trying to see the source of the noise.

I felt myself go cold all over. I wanted to run, and felt silly. I was sure my legs wouldn't do anything I told them to do just then.

Something seemed to be coming directly at us. Whatever it was, it stayed low, seemed to hug the undergrowth for cover. I worried it might be a bear or something, because of the rocks behind us, maybe heading for a den and we just happened to be in its path. But it didn't growl or give a warning like a wild animal would. Not at first.

Then it did start to make noises, crying noises. Like a child. A panther, I thought. A panther is said to sound just like a baby crying.

All of a sudden, I saw her emerging from out of the brush. She did cry, but she wasn't an animal. Least, not a four-legged kind.

She looked about six years old, and she wore a homespun dress, dirty, tattered along the hem. Her hair appeared dark in the moonlight and tossed about so, I thought at first she was one of those wild children my daddy used to warn us about, the ones who had no momma nor daddy and ran around the mountain, mostly nurtured by some wild animal that took pity on their hunger and loneliness. But the tears in her eyes told me she was just lost and confused and probably as scared as we were.

"My goodness! It's a little girl," Hannah Jane said. She stood up halfway, preparing to run over to the child, when John Croshaw caught her by the hand and pulled her back down.

"Don't," he said. "It's a trick. She's one of them." He bent over and picked up a rock.

"Go away," he said to the girl. He cocked his arm as if he were about to toss the rock at her.

"What are you doing?" Hannah Jane and I said, almost in unison. Before we finished our question, the little girl turned and ran back into the brush.

John Croshaw looked at us and said, "What are you staring at? It's a trick! It's how they lure other children into their trap. She's one of them. I know it."

"Well, I don't know it," I said. "She didn't look like anything but a scared kid. She looked . . . she looked just like us."

He threw the rock down to the ground. "Then, go after her yourself, if you think she's like us. Go ahead, Chester. Go on, take your whining self with you and don't come back—"

I interrupted. "That's enough, sir. I am going after her." I looked at Hannah Jane. I wanted to say, *I'm sorry I won't be able to keep my promise to stay with you,* but there wasn't time. Instead, I said to John Croshaw, "You take care of Hannah Jane . . . or else. . . ." I didn't finish because I couldn't think of *or else what.*

"Ches—" Hannah Jane started to say something to me.

I didn't let her finish. "I'll catch up with you later. Meet both of you at Devil's Head."

John Croshaw said, "Right, Chester, you meet us at Devil's Head. Bring the little vampire girl with you. If she lets you. Who knows? You could be her next meal. They have unnatural strength and power, you know. Don't worry about Hannah Jane. She's where she belongs."

I didn't answer. I couldn't think of anything to say. I started into the woods in the direction of the girl.

"Let's hurry," I heard him say to Hannah Jane. "She'll probably tell the others where we are." Then he called out to me, "Chester, when they capture you, tell them we're safe at Devil's Head." He laughed.

I didn't think it was all that funny.

CHAPTER EIGHT

And so alone, so far from home,
I shuffle through the snow,
And hear the sounds that make hearts pound
And still have miles to go.

I NEVER FELT SO ALONE in my entire life. Every noise sounded like an alien. Or an animal who was going to jump out from its hiding place and eat me.

The woods grew deeper where the little girl had gone. I didn't have the heavy snow to reveal her footsteps. Wasn't long till I became lost. Fact is, I was lost the moment I went after her. At least John Croshaw wasn't along to point it out.

I started to lose control. I could see only a few yards in front of me. Anyone who thinks it's quiet in the woods should try it at night. Creatures who wouldn't be caught dead in daylight come out after dark. Looking for something to eat, mainly. I wondered how tasty I looked to whatever it was that had just rustled in a thicket next to me. I stopped.

So did whatever I heard.

My heart started pounding again. I backed against a giant tulip tree and tried to catch my breath.

Times like this, my mind always seemed to wander to a better place. Home. Daddy puttering. Working on his project in the tool-shed out back of the house. Windmills from kitchen matches, ash-trays put together with old tin cans and baling wire. He always liked to give them away to the smokers at the machine shop where he had worked since he and my mother married when they were still teenagers. I could hear Momma harping on his mess. I could hear him saying something like *Sit down*.

"Sit down," I heard him say. Daddy's voice. So clear in my head, I almost expected to look up and he would be there. He was not. I could hear him all the same. Only, he wasn't talking to Momma. He was talking to me.

"Sit down, boy! Catch your bearings. Just 'cause you're lost, don't mean it's over."

He'd told me many times what to do if I was to get lost in the woods. Pointed it out on our little trips when we would take off from home to see how far we could walk of a morning. His instructions came back clear to me now. Clear as his gray eyes and just as bright.

"Sit down, first," he would tell me. "Sit yourself down and rest. Ain't no use wearing yourself out. Catch your bearings. Take a look up at the sky. You know where home is from the sun by day, the stars by night. Cloudy nights, and you can't see the stars, look at the trees. Look where the moss grows. That's the north side."

I felt behind me for the growth. Sure enough. Found it a little to my right. And the stars? I would be able to see them when the clouds passed. He had pointed them out to me often enough. "Up there, way yonder, see, that's the North Star. Polaris, they call it. And right there, looks like a ladle, that one's. . . ."

The sky had looked magic to me then. A whole other world of bear and horse and archer and more mysteries than a fellow could count in a lifetime. He drew maps in the dirt. I think Daddy liked the stars because they gave him something to dream about. A short, compact man, like me, he always had tall dreams, tall as the sky, bright as the stars. Tall dreams, for sure. Putterers like to dream while they putter. I always saw them in his eyes. The dreams, I mean. Dreams twinkling like the stars.

"Go downhill," Daddy would say. "Find running water. Follow it downhill. People and livestock drink water. Follow the stream downhill. You'll soon find houses and people who can get you pointed to home."

I felt better. "Thanks, all the same, Daddy," I said, pretending he sat right in front of me, "except this time, downhill is the direction of the aliens." Soon as I said the word, I felt a shiver across my shoulders. I knew what I would have to do.

The look on my daddy's face got serious now, because he knew I would choose to disregard his advice.

"I'm sorry," I said, "but this time I'm going uphill, not down." I looked over in the direction I supposed Devil's Head to be.

Daddy looked downright agitated. But he wasn't stuck up there on that cold mountainside, and I was.

I cut back to near where I'd left off the trail. Then I angled up some, so I wouldn't run into someone I didn't want to meet up with. I found the going hard, but I had a purpose: catching up with Hannah Jane.

After an hour, Devil's Head rose up before me. It hovered across a deep gorge—not all that far from me as the crow flies, but a couple miles of hard climbing from where I had left the trail. The sides fell off the crest almost like a cliff. I would not be able to cut the butter and cross straight over to the safety of the ridge. Not if I could believe John Croshaw. I decided to circle up, to sneak up Devil's Head from behind. It would take twice the time, but the only other way led down.

In the middle of my decision-making, the clouds parted. To my surprise, I saw Hannah Jane and John Croshaw in the distance, far away on the other side of the gorge. They were only a few yards from their destination, running like crazy across a rocky opening some twenty yards from the ridge itself. They reminded me of ants caught in a trapdoor spider hole, the way they scratched and struggled against the loose gravel leading up to the ridge. Finally, John Croshaw made it to the rim and reached back for Hannah Jane. He took hold of her hand and pulled her over, and I found myself both happy and sad.

Happy she was safe. And at the same time, fighting a nagging feeling that maybe this might be the last time I would see her again. "King's X," I whispered, praying they really had reached safety.

After an hour and a half, I came upon the back side of the ridge. I almost called out for my lost companions, then choked down the words. I thought better of it, not wanting to reveal my location to someone I didn't want to find me.

The mountaintop deceived anyone observing it from a distance. From below, it looked barren and rocky, as if nothing could grow there. At the top, I discovered the opposite. Over the other side of the rocky ridge called Devil's Head, which runs about two miles long, lies a large, circular plateau, the center of an ancient volcano.

Red spruce and balsam fir, first-generation trees, untouched giants, towered over me as I picked my way toward the place where I estimated I had last caught sight of Hannah Jane and John Croshaw. I felt more secure now, almost peaceful. The moon still hid behind moving clouds, but I didn't have to struggle with the thick rhododendrons, mountain laurel, or fetterbush undergrowth that blocked my way on the trail below the rim. I had my bearings now, thanks to Daddy. I knew it would be only a matter of time before I found the rim of the plateau.

I was certain I would discover Hannah Jane and John Croshaw there. We would wait until morning, then walk out, safe and sound. At least, that's what Momma Opalona had led me to believe those many years before.

"They hates the light of day," she'd said. "Can't tolerate the sunshine. Like all true vampires, they very bodies shrivels up and wastes away in the daylight."

I didn't care what John Croshaw would say to that. I was getting out of there come morning. Hannah Jane would be coming with me.

I stumbled upon a mountain stream and knelt down to wash my face. Icy water revived me. I took the time to eat one of the sandwiches I had almost forgotten in my knapsack. I had one soda left, drank it, and put the empty bottle back in my pack. Up there in that virgin forest, I had a feeling trash would spoil its beauty. I was glad I felt that way, grateful my daddy had taken me with him on his trips into the woods.

"I want you to see things the way they ought to be," he'd said, teaching me to leave nature the way I found it. I was in the middle of congratulating myself, when I heard the sound of something coming in my direction.

I crawled behind a low, flat, moss-covered rock, long as my body, with a small overhang so I could squeeze into its shadow. I listened. Whoever they were, they were coming along the stream from a trail just above and parallel to me. From the sound their footsteps made, there were many, walking as if they had nothing to fear. I craned my neck around the rock. I couldn't see them. But I did see my knapsack, next to the stream, out in the open for someone to trip over. I reached out and grabbed it, just as the first one came into sight, walking on my side of the stream. For a moment I froze, not believing what I had seen. I jerked my head back behind the rock and started to pray.

I could still visualize it in my imagination, like when you close your eyes and something bright stays there, framed in your mind as if your eyes were still open. Its face glowed like a dim lightbulb. The head was partially covered by a long silky cloak with a hood that pulled down over its . . . I would say eyes, but I didn't see any. What I saw was a ghostly, filtered glow coming from a round face that contained no features. Equally formless hands extended out of the sleeves of the cloak. No fingers. At first, I thought the creature wore mittens, but the hands glowed like the face. That was all I saw clearly. There were figures following behind the thing, but I didn't make them out.

I did hear them. It seemed forever, though it was only a minute or so. They passed my hiding place, going downstream, in the direction where I figured Hannah Jane and John Croshaw thought they would be safe. A flash of anger crossed my mind. So much for John Croshaw's daddy. Then fear replaced anger.

I waited till I could hear them no more, then I ran. Ran in the opposite direction of the creatures who had almost caught me off guard. I ran without watching where my feet came down, not concerned that I might fall or hurt myself. My only concern? Distance, putting myself as far away from them as I could. I ran until I fell down. I got up and ran some more. And then I stopped.

I could hear Daddy: "Boy, when you run away from something, you're only gonna find the same thing when you get to where you're going."

"Yeah, but, Daddy. . . ."

I sat down and rubbed the tears off my face. I could hear Daddy telling his favorite story about Uncle Joe, my momma's brother, who chased Japanese submarines from an airplane in the Pacific when he was in the war.

"One day," Daddy said, "your Uncle Joe was out with some of his war buddies, hunting grizzly bears in Alaska, where he was stationed when he was in the Navy. Well, it didn't go all that well because, you see, a bear is just about the cunningest critter in the woods. So, that grizzly took to stalking the hunters themselves. Pretty soon, he shows himself and growls and starts to charge them hunters. Well, they all run. All, every one of them. Except your Uncle Joe. Joe stands his ground, and that grizzly takes note of that, and he pulls up to see what Uncle Joe's gonna do next."

I had this story memorized because, up to now, I could not think of a situation so fearful as being stalked by a bear. I always wondered how I would react.

Uncle Joe had stood his ground, and when the grizzly decided to charge for real, my uncle knelt down on one knee, took aim, and shot that bear down.

"Took him three shots," Daddy said, "the last no more than ten yards, and the bear slumped down for the last time." Of that, Daddy observed, "I reckon there are times to run, for sure. But

when the time comes you can't run fast enough to escape yourself, you ought to think about taking a stand."

If I was going to warn Hannah Jane and John Croshaw, I would
have to hurry, circling around again, hopefully arriving at the rim
before the aliens, or whatever they were.

I must have made it just in time. Hannah Jane and John
Croshaw were resting in the middle of an open meadow, surrounded by the same trees where I now hid. Just as I was about
to run out into the clearing to warn them, I sensed movement a
few yards to my right. I stopped, trying to decide whether I should
call out a warning and risk giving myself away. I made a decision to
wait it out and try to figure out the situation. It occurred to me
that I might soon be the only one left to slip down the mountain
for help. What I saw next made my heart drop down into my
stomach.

Hannah Jane and John Croshaw lay on the grassy field. John
Croshaw had his arms around her.

Rats, I thought. *They're necking.*

Only, she screamed and slapped him.

Serves him right, I decided, *trying to take favors with my girl.*

She screamed again and tried to run from him. No luck. He had
her around the wrist, his hand like a vice. She tried pushing him
again, slapping, fighting.

The thought hadn't come to me yet to run out to help her. And
when it did, I thought of the others who lurked in the woods just
out of my sight. The whole scene left me stunned. Just then, I knew
something was very wrong. It wasn't just John Croshaw. My whole
body went numb with the realization of it. . . .

The others had come out of the woods by now, and they began to
gather around Hannah Jane and John Croshaw. My attention still
focused on Hannah Jane's struggle. Some time passed before I got
a good look at them. My first impulse? To run away again. I stopped
myself and considered sacrificing myself to help Hannah Jane.
Something in the back of my mind held me in place. Fear or reason,
I knew not, but I came to the conclusion that the only way I could
save her was to force myself to watch and report what I saw. Then
I would follow them to their hiding place.

She screamed again. Her screams turned to tears. I had never
seen Hannah Jane cry. Not even when she fell from a horse she had
been trying to ride and broke a wrist so bad the bones ruptured

through her skin and she bit her lower lip till they took her to the doctor. Not when her momma and daddy decided they could no longer live together and moved apart. Not even. . . .

She cried now and she begged, "Please, Johnny, don't let them hurt me."

I rubbed the tears from my own eyes. A deep flush worked its way to my face, and the woods seemed to turn around me. I kept telling myself that I could not pass out, that I had to witness the cruelty before me, that if I did not report what I had seen, no one would ever know.

She freed one of her arms and hit him in the eye. I felt like cheering her on, but I stayed still.

John Croshaw recovered and held her tighter. The others had formed a circle around the two of them as they struggled there on the ground. That's when I got a better look at the others.

I shouldn't have been surprised to discover they weren't all aliens. I counted only ten who wore the silky cloaks. The others? Children. All ages. Different races. I saw black children and those who were Native American. Cherokee, I decided, from the pictures I had seen in history books. Two Orientals looked like brother and sister. The little girl with light hair and a homespun dress stood there. John Croshaw had not lied about that. She was one of them. It struck me suddenly that some of the children were dressed in old-fashioned clothes, as if they had not come from my own time.

It was like Momma Opalona had reported, that children had been missing since just after the War Between the States. That would make it the late 1860s, I calculated. If Momma Opalona was right, some of those children have been like that almost a hundred years. I stopped calculating when I saw what happened next.

Hannah Jane wouldn't shut up. Now she had regained some of her composure and threatened John Croshaw. "My poppa's gonna whup you so you can't sit down for life if you don't let me go, now!"

He ignored her. He just kept saying, "They won't hurt you, Hannah Jane. It won't hurt at all."

"It already does, Johnny." She still called him Johnny. "You're hurting me something awful. Now let me go! I promise I won't tell nobody. Let go of me!"

I felt like a knife had cut me in two. I wanted to run out to help Hannah Jane, but I heard the smart part of me say, *It's up to you, Chester. You can run out there, raise a ruckus, and get captured, doing nobody any good. Or, you can hang tough and find a way to get down the mountain for help.* I decided I had to use my head instead of my heart.

By this time, the circle of aliens and children around Hannah Jane and John Croshaw was complete. I estimated close to a hundred. Between every tenth child, an alien stood. They held hands like some kind of kid's game, only it didn't look like play to me. Hannah Jane kept screaming, pushing, and threatening. One of the aliens walked into the center where she lay, kicking against John Croshaw. The alien pulled what looked like two lengths of tubing out from under his cloak. Each ran about four feet long, and the ends had a needle, a good three inches. That's when I noticed everyone else, except John Croshaw, had tubes just like the aliens. I watched as they all inserted the needles into their arms.

I regretted eating my sandwich when my stomach told me it was going to let go any minute. I held it in, almost passing out from the pain. A cold sweat broke over my body. I pulled my mackinaw up around my neck and just wanted to go to sleep and wake to find I'd had a terrible nightmare. But I didn't fall asleep. What happened next kept me wide awake.

Hannah Jane must have known the end was near, because she stopped screaming. I heard her sob as the alien bent over and pushed the needles into her arms. She screamed again. When they finished, the whole bunch of them stood in a circle, their arms connected one to the other by the tubes. Hannah Jane, John Croshaw, the children, and aliens, all formed the circle. Everyone seemed to be waiting. The aliens looked up into the sky. They watched, still as death. Even Hannah Jane seemed frozen. I decided it was from fear.

They waited till the clouds moved from the moon, and all the aliens raised and lowered their arms, allowing their cloaks to fall from their milky bodies. They began to make a noise like the sound of a motor vibrating. It got louder. I realized it wasn't a motor at all. More like the noise a cat makes when it's purring. That's it, I decided. They were all purring.

I felt the vibration from where I hid. All of a sudden, Hannah Jane screamed again, and I saw why. Those white bodies became transparent. You could see right through them. Only, they weren't empty. They were filled with thousands of crisscrossing veins— just that, nothing more. The veins lit up, and what I saw almost made me pee in my trousers. Blood, blue-colored blood, ran through their veins. I didn't have to imagine where they got it.

Then, just as it had started, it ended. The aliens removed the tubes and cloaked themselves. Everyone got disconnected, lined up behind one of the aliens, and started back into the woods from where they had come.

Hannah Jane did the same as the rest. She no longer resisted. Whatever had happened to her, it made her as passive as the other children. I wanted to call out to her, get her attention so we could slip out together. It was like a dream. The girl I loved was now under an influence I could not begin to understand.

I felt dizzy again, about to pass out, when it came to me: I'd been holding my breath, so I'd forgotten to breathe. I still felt sick, knowing it wasn't over. I would have to follow them to wherever it was they hid themselves.

It was downhill a bit. John Croshaw hadn't lied about that. Still, I wondered who had been chasing us—the men with weapons. I would worry about that later.

Following them required no effort. They had nothing to fear, no lookouts to cover their trail. I stayed a safe distance behind and watched them walk along the creek until they arrived at a rock formation. They walked into it and disappeared.

Sure, I told myself, *now either you're seeing things, or they can walk through rocks.*

I was right: I was seeing things.

Up near the boulders, a trail led down between two stone formations, tall as the biggest beech tree I'd ever seen, well over a hundred and fifty feet. A narrow opening, just large enough for a body to pass through and over a hundred feet long, led into the black mouth of a cave. That's as far as I went. I had the feeling, if I went any farther, I wouldn't come out. Not as a human, leastwise.

I estimated the time. Near five in the morning. Daylight began to break over the horizon. My problems were just beginning.

PART II
The Journey

CHAPTER NINE

If you find you got to tell a tale,
Tell it to the man in jail.

THEY GRABBED ME on the way down. The men who had been following us on the way up. Deputy sheriffs. Took no time to haul me into jail.

"What have you done with my daughter?" Hannah Jane's mother screamed. Her house duster and hair—put up in pins—looked out of place for such a tidy person. But the woman took no note of her appearance just then. Her voice screamed anger, and frustration, and hatred for me. And fear for her daughter.

Hannah Jane's father showed up later at the sheriff's office. He told the sheriff my life wasn't worth a plug nickel—or words to that effect.

The sheriff finally sent for my parents. Small favors.

Momma never minced words. "Our oldest boy is crazy, Emmett!" I heard her voice through the door of the interrogation room where they put me after the deputies took me into the jail, once they got past Hannah Jane's family and the merely curious who gathered outside the jailhouse.

I was alone again. Nothing to keep me company but a table, two chairs, and a ceiling fan that vibrated like it was about to fly off on its own somewhere.

Daddy took my side, sorta. I wondered if they knew I could hear them in the hallway. "He's okay, Hazel, just a little confused from being lost up there on that mountain."

I recognized the sheriff's voice the second I heard it. Deep and gravelly, just like the one I'd heard up on Devil's Mountain when I thought we were being chased by aliens. Only, it hadn't been aliens chasing us. John Croshaw knew that. That's why he worked so hard to get away from them. He figured it out. It was the sheriff and his deputies, tipped off by Hannah Jane's blabbermouth sister, Margaret Anne, who told her parents, who told the sheriff, who put together a posse, which chased us all over Devil's Mountain before being led off the trail by a little girl who acted like she was lost. They lost her too.

The door burst open and the three of them entered: Daddy, Momma, and the sheriff. Momma had put on the same calico dress she always wore when she had to go somewhere in a hurry. Daddy wore his usual work overalls, laced-up boots, and plaid wool cap that was as old as I was. The sheriff told them they could take a chair next to me. He stood over all of us, pulling on his suspenders, to which he had pinned a tarnished brass star inscribed with the words SHERIFF OF TRANSYLVANIA COUNTY surrounding the seal of the State of North Carolina.

He took off his fedora, and sweat rolled off the top of his head, where the last few strands of his red hair hung on for dear life. The furrows in his forehead contracted when he looked at me. Momma held a handkerchief to catch the tears, and Daddy tried to keep up my spirits by smiling.

The sheriff leaned on the table directly across from me. He said, "Chester, I know you had a bad time up there, but you gotta tell us what really happened so we can find the other two children and get you the help you need." He didn't sound angry or anything. I got the feeling he did want to help.

I felt caught. Caught between the truth, as I knew it, and the sheriff's own suspicions of what he believed had happened. I knew there was nothing I could say that would make him, or anyone, believe me. So I answered him the only way I could. I told the truth.

When I finished my story, I told him, "It all happened like I said, Sheriff. Just like I said."

The sheriff came back at me in a hurry. "Boy, is there a word of truth in any of that nonsense you've been making up?" All of a sudden, he didn't sound so caring. When he spoke again, his voice stretched tighter, like he was about to lose his temper. "Now, you had just better tell me the truth, Chester, or I'm gonna throw you in jail." He emphasized the word *jail*, drawing it out loud and long, so I got the message he was serious.

I wanted to explain to him about Momma Opalona, and what John Croshaw had said about his daddy and all, but when I started on that, he got even angrier. "Now don't go putting it all off on the other boy, Chester. We already know things don't square with him. We looked for his house, to tell his folks he's missing, and all we found was an abandoned sharecropper shack and a parcel of clothes what matches stuff stolen from the dry goods store."

I shook my head. "Don't that prove he was in on it, that he was one of them, you know, like I said?"

The sheriff put his face square in front of mine so I could almost feel the heat from his breath and the smell of tobacco and Juicy Fruit gum. He narrowed his eyes and spoke in a whisper, like what he had to say was something real important. "Chester, we know he was in on it. But he ain't here and you are." He raised his voice so my parents could hear, as well. "Now, what did you boys do with that girl?"

He looked over my head, straight at my parents. I could see that his eyes remained narrowed. When he spoke this time, his voice was so strained I could tell he had reached the limits of his patience. "You better get your boy to tell the truth now, or he's going straight to jail and gonna stay there till he does."

Momma started crying again, and Daddy put his arm around her. "Now, Hazel," he said, "you stop that. It's gonna be all right, now. You wait and see. It's all gonna work out." Daddy believed me. At least, he believed I didn't hurt anyone. He also believed I was "confused" when all I had to say was that I saw alien vampires turn Hannah Jane into one of them, just like John Croshaw.

That didn't stop Momma from crying, nor did it prevent the sheriff from threatening to throw me in jail. He said he was thinking about charging me with kidnapping—or worse—if I didn't let on that I knew where the bodies were. Bodies?

He came up with his final offer: "Young man, you look me right in the eyes now so's you can see I mean what I'm about to tell you." He paused for effect. "You got twenty-four hours to come clean, or I'm a-sending you off to jail for good."

I could tell by the look in his eyes, he meant every word.

CHAPTER TEN

A ghost, a ghost, I think almost
I saw a ghost tonight.
I'm not sure where, the alley there,
I saw a ghost in flight.

FIRST, I THOUGHT I was seeing things for sure. I told myself it had to be the strain of the last twenty-four hours. Then I reflected on the next twenty-four hours and decided it must have been my imagination. I could not have seen John Croshaw, lurking like a ghost in the shadows of the alley next to the jail, as I left with my parents to go home and pray for a miracle.

For prayer was all we had just then. Funny, how folks all tend to go into themselves when a tragedy strikes. Momma and Daddy paced in and out of the house most of the evening, meeting on the front porch where they could trade their secret misgivings so as not to frighten Aldous and me. Finally, Momma called us all together at the kitchen table for the food no one wanted to eat.

Daddy didn't start it off on too high a note when he offered, "Chester, there's folks who say that jail ain't all that bad."

Momma gave him her special stare, which only egged Daddy on. "Yessir," he said. "I knew a fella down Asheville who put on near forty pounds on prison food. Why, I tell you, boy—"

She broke into tears and got out a choke-filled "Emmett, this ain't helping none."

He plowed ahead. "Honey, he gotta take this like a man. Now you know—"

Momma rose so hard, her chair went flying backwards. Pretty soon, we could hear her tears coming from the bedroom. I saw the pain in Daddy's eyes. Pain for Momma, for her tears, for her loss. He looked at me, and I read the message in his eyes: *You can do it, boy.* No words. Words would have watered down the message. Our food grew as cold as our hearts just then.

In time, he stood up and walked toward the bedroom, speaking a plaintive "Honey, you okay?" that sounded as helpless as his ability to make things right for her.

It was then that something went off inside of me and I knew for a-certain that Daddy had to be right. I would do it, whatever the *it* meant. Times are, you have to do it all by yourself.

Aldous fidgeted in bed, from time to time looking over at me all supine with my open eyes straight up trying to remember what the watermarks in the ceiling wallpaper used to mean to me when I was a kid. *There's the ghost*, I recalled.

My mind went back to the morning, to the alley. Had I seen a ghost for sure? Or a monster? John Croshaw? Of course, the clouds on the ceiling looked like ghosts, and monsters, and angels, and. . . .

My brother sat up in bed. "I been remembering," he said.

"That right?"

"Yeah, remembering."

"Okay." I waited, but he lay back down, and I allowed my mind to drift off somewhere else, somewhere in the past, when the morning would not bring sadness.

Aldous sat up again. "I was thinking about the time those boys surrounded us on the baseball field after practice. Remember?"

"Yes."

"They said they was going to take away our balls and our bats and our gloves. Remember?"

I waited for him to make his point.

"Remember, Chester? Do you remember?"

"Yes, I remember."

"Know what I remember?"

"No, Aldous, I don't know what you remember."

"I remember how they acted all tough and such, and how they said as how they was gonna take away our balls and bats and such, and there was nothing we could do about it. Do you remember that?"

"Yes, I do."

"But that ain't what I really remember."

"It ain't?"

"No sir, Chess, that is not what I remember. I remember how you said we should take our stand there and not run. I remember how, when you saw them coming, you told me that they was up to no good and that we ought to hold our ground and not give up without a fight, and I remember how that sorta made them wonder that maybe we wouldn't be all that easy for them to scare, and I remember how they looked at us when they started to reach for our stuff, and we didn't move, so they couldn't be sure whether we would fight them or not, and I remember how they seen we didn't run, so they just kinda decided it might not be worth picking a fight if we was to fight them back, and how—"

"Aldous."

"Yeah?"

"Why are you telling me this?"

He paused, his eyes wide, head cocked. "Don't ya see, Chess?"

"What am I missing?"

"Why, it's just the same now. Don't ya see? They got you surrounded, see. Only, you ain't gonna give them no reason to think you're afraid. Are you, Chess?"

Little brothers. How they remind you of the lessons you teach them. Up to that point, jail had been the greatest fear of my life—until Aldous made me remember.

CHAPTER ELEVEN

In the dark of the woods
Dwells a dream, dream, dream,
Watching walkers walk, walk
Where the wild things seem.

I DREAMT I SAW HIM AGAIN. John Croshaw, I mean. In the woods. I dreamt I saw him in the woods when the prison bus took a turn and had to slow down real slow. There he stood, clear as glass. Must have been a dream. He stared at me, his eyes fixed on my presence, as if he had been waiting for me, expecting me to drive on by just then. He watched me, all chained up in that bus, on my way to what the sheriff referred to as jail.

Must have been a dream.

Jail was the North Carolina Reformatory, a cluster of old army quonset huts that once housed a National Guard armory. The detention center sat in the middle of a wide grassy cove, cut out of a hardwood forest of white basswood, sweet buckeye, tulip tree, sugar maple, yellow birch, beech, and eastern hemlock, with a sprinkling of bitternut hickory, red oak, white oak, and cucumber magnolia. I know because I made a mental note of every one of them, on my three-hour-long bus ride to the reform school that was to be my home a lot longer than I would have believed.

If it hadn't been for the fence, I would have loved it there. The forest grew beautiful as any I had seen in the Appalachian Mountains. But the reformatory kept me from those trees, and the fact that I could only look made it all the harder on me.

A twelve-foot-high chain-link fence, topped with razor wire, enclosed the camp. Inside the perimeter lay a "D" line. The warden called it that. "D" stood for "dead," which meant that if you stepped across the line, an officer in a front gate tower would radio a pickup truck full of armed officers, who would show up to "shoot you down like the dirty dogs you are," to quote the warden.

The warden was not a big man. He was almost as short as me, with thin white hair, cut short, except on the top where he left it long, so he could comb it over his bald spot. His face found a way to squeeze itself together, so you couldn't even see his eyes. He reminded me of someone sucking on a lemon. When he talked, he pointed his finger to emphasize what he said. Everything must have been important, because he pointed a lot. He wore the same khaki uniform all the correctional officers wore—only, his was loose and baggy. And his badge was bigger—and golden colored instead of silver. He spoke with a high-pitched, whiny twang. When he paused to think, he made an *eeeeehhhh* sound and crinkled his nose like he had just smelled something bad. A brown stain from spit tobacco had taken up permanent residence on the corners of his mouth, and I took notice of the tip of the finger he used to point with, since the tobacco stain from his cigarette had dyed his fingernail a permanent reddish brown.

While he read the rules to me from across his desk, I became distracted by his office, which looked like a jungle. The warden was partial to potted plants—all kinds of plants—but most of all, he favored spider plants, which hung down from hooks in the ceiling, their little tentacles touching almost to the floor.

"Ain't you paying no attention at all?" he said to me.

"Yes, sir."

"Then suppose *you* recite back to *me* the last rule *I* read to *you*." There was something else I noticed about his voice. He always emphasized the pronouns in his speech.

"Well, sir. . . ."

"I didn't think you were paying no attention." He smiled, but it wasn't a friendly smile. "Well, that's okay, because nobody never pays no attention to the rules, first time. That's why they have to go on over to that cell there"—he pointed out the window behind him to a small brick building in the middle of the compound—"and write down these-here rules in this-here notebook." He pulled a Big Chief tablet out of his desk and threw it at me, along with a small blue booklet. "It will take some time. So, I suppose you won't mind not getting nothing to eat till breakfast. Unless, of course, you don't get your punishment done by then. Do you understand?"

"Yes, sir."

He smiled again, still not friendly. Then he opened a brown manila folder that had my name on it and started reading. I could tell he was reading, because his lips moved and he traced his finger along the page.

"Says here, you ain't charged with nothing yet. Says here, you are uncooperative." It took him a long time to sound out the word. When he finished, he looked crosswise at the folder, then up at me. "I suppose that means you ain't all right in the head." He pointed his finger to his head and spun it around while he stuck his tongue out of his mouth and made some kind of garbled sounds.

I laughed, which I shouldn't have done, because he suddenly got a serious look on his face. He leaned forward, staring at me. He said, "You think that's funny, don't you?"

"No, sir."

"You know what we do to prisoners who don't take this-here place seriously?"

"No, sir."

He started smiling again. "We put them in the hole, that's what."

I was soon to learn that two cells had been designated for isolation of boys who needed special discipline. They were called the hole because it was supposed to be like being isolated from the rest of the prisoners.

The warden explained, "You don't take this place seriously, we take away your privileges and put you in isolation. Now, do you still think this here's a funny place?"

By this time, my head hung down so my chin touched my chest. "No, sir," I said, and for the first time since what started out as a joke turned into a matter of life and death, I felt like I had to fight back my tears.

The warden must have seen that, because he laid right into me. "Don't you cry, boy. You cry, and you go to the hole right away."

"I ain't gonna cry," I said. *No way I'm going to give you the satisfaction*, I thought.

The correctional officer led me to the brick building, which turned out to be a small classroom with student desks, a blackboard, and nothing else, not even a teacher's desk. "You go do what the warden says, now, hear me?"

He pulled the door behind him, leaving me standing there hungry and alone. I heard the key turn in the lock and his footsteps fade away. It was seven in the evening. By that time, the blue rule book looked three inches thick.

"This is going to take me all night," I whispered. I hadn't eaten since a breakfast of cold scrambled eggs and dry white toast at the Transylvania County Jail.

My mind wandered for a time back to Devil's Mountain. Hannah Jane. Was she still. . . ?

"No time to think on that," I whispered. "You got a job to do, Chess." I sat down at one of the desks, opened the book of rules, put my pencil to the tablet, and tried to keep my mind off my stomach.

CHAPTER TWELVE

If life's a long, long row to hoe,
Sometimes a body has got to say no!

I HADN'T EATEN more than a few scraps in the three days since I got there. Not for lack of food. More than enough food to fill me. Only, I never figured out how to eat it fast enough. By the time I got to my table in the mess hall, the food on my platter was scraped off by boys bigger than me.

The mess hall had twenty-five metal tables bolted to the floor. Four round, metal, stool-type seats jutted out on extension rods welded to the center pole of each table. Ingenious engineering. Made sure no one ever got mad and decided to throw a chair or table at someone. Fact is, everyone was too busy eating to get into a fight.

I changed that.

By the time I got to my table on the fourth day, I had made up my mind. No one would ever take my food from my plate again. I wasn't completely successful, but I did manage to save a couple of scoopfuls of rice and my chocolate pudding by the time I sat down. I considered it a feast. Well, almost.

I was about to bite down on my first spoonful of rice, when Joe Ray McQuarter started in my direction. I understood his intentions because, the day before, when I was about to eat a piece of bread I kept concealed during the scavenging by the other boys, Joe Ray walked up to my table, took the bread out of my hand, and used it to sponge up the last bit of gravy on his platter. Now he was coming back for seconds.

"Not this time," I mumbled, leaning over my food to protect it with my body.

Joe Ray looked down on me. He stood big, over six feet, eighteen years old—the maximum age for boys at the reformatory. Joe Ray looked older because of the long, blond, scraggly whiskers hanging off his chin. His hair brushed across his blue eyes, which he squinted at me to indicate he meant business. His breath smelled as bad as the rest of him.

"Gimme that!" he said. Joe Ray was not a man of many words.

"No!"

He reached down with his big bony hands and pulled at my platter. He didn't want the bread this time. He wanted it all.

"No!" I said, gritting my teeth. "It's mine!"

By then, the officers in charge of the mess looked at us, but none of them moved to do anything. I was on my own.

"Gimme that food, or I'll beat you up," he whispered in my ear.

A full sentence. I was impressed, but I did not relent. "It's mine, and you can't have it," I whispered right back. I was in for it. I knew it. But I had taken about all I could. We pulled at both ends of the platter like dogs fighting over a bone. Something had to give.

It did.

He was stronger, so after a few tugs, the tray slipped out of my grasp, sending gravy and scraps all over Joe Ray's face, followed immediately by the thump of the tray on his nose.

"There, you can have it all," I said. The irony of the situation had not yet caught up to me. I couldn't have hurt him more if I had been able to whip him. All the other boys, and even the officers, started laughing at Joe Ray, standing there all covered in gravy, rice, and chocolate pudding.

I laughed, too, on my way to the hole.

Joe Ray walked on the other side of the officer, telling me all the time what he was going to do to me when we got out.

I didn't want out. It wasn't because of Joe Ray, either. In the hole, I got to eat all I wanted, and I met the boy who was to be my friend for life.

He was not much taller than me. His hair had grown dirty-blond, and he had green eyes. He didn't seem imposing at first, till I took note of a wild look about him that told me he was used to taking care of himself. I found out I was right, but it wasn't as simple as I thought.

His name, I learned later, was Gary Wayne Kirk. Sent to isolation for talking back to one of the officers. He had to room with me because there were only two isolation cells, and he refused to bunk with Joe Ray "'cause his breath smells almost as bad as the rest of him."

Our cell was a seven-by-twelve room secured by a steel door with a tiny window so they could watch us. A food slot allowed the stewards to pass our trays into the cell without opening the door. Inside the gray cinder-block room, two steel bunks, one over the other, had been bolted to the wall. A lavatory and toilet took up one corner. No windows to the outside world. I saw right away, I would miss my view of the woods. But the semi-privacy and food would more than make up for the view. We had a choice to sleep on top of the cotton tick, two-inch-thick mattresses, or under them for cover. Either way, we froze: from the bottom, if we slept on the hard steel bunk, or on top, if we left the mattress under us.

For two days, not a word passed between us. Finally, I broke the silence. "What you in for?" It sounded stupid, soon as I said it.

He didn't take kindly to the question. He looked at me sideways, then said, "Ain't supposed to ask no one that. Ain't supposed to ask a body what he's in here for."

I said, "I don't know the rules here, except what the warden made me write out."

"He makes all of us do that."

"Wasn't anything in there about not asking someone what he's in for."

"Not one of the warden's rules. It's sorta like an unwritten rule."

"I don't suppose you'd like to tell me any other unwritten rules," I said.

He did.

Gary Wayne told me how the hundred boys who lived in the reformatory were placed there for things as bad as murder or as simple as being a runaway. He said that if you were a "fish"—that's what they called a new kid—you would be tested till you fought back. He said that the best thing I did was to stand up to Joe Ray. He said it was also the worst thing I did, since Joe Ray was in for almost beating another kid to death in an argument over a girl—or so he boasted to everyone in earshot as often as he could.

And he told me how the system works so you get time off for good behavior, or "Good Time" as it's called. Of course, I had no idea how much time I had to serve, since I hadn't exactly been sentenced.

"Do you play chess?" he then asked me.

"Well, no," I said, "but what good would it be if I did. We don't have a game board in here."

Gary Wayne laughed. "Got to make do," he said. "Look over yonder." He pointed to the toilet paper. "Long as we got that, we got us a chess board."

I never knew so much could be done with toilet paper. In a couple of hours, we made a board and chess figures good enough for Gary Wayne to begin the patient process of teaching me how to play the game. By the end of the week, I had learned to play well enough to make it interesting for him. I also learned about the boy who helped me survive.

"I didn't break no law or nothing," Gary Wayne said. "Just took back what was rightly mine."

"Took back what?"

"My motor scooter."

"Motor scooter?"

"Yeah, little red Cushman. Not much to shout about, but it got me to school and work and all. Didn't need no license to drive it. Rode all over the place, free as a bird. Used to work on it with my daddy till . . . until he passed away. Momma said I had to go and stay a time with my gramma and grandpa on the Georgia border over near the Chattahoochee Forest."

"You lived with your grandparents?"

"That's right, till Momma got over. . . . Well, she didn't take it all too well, Daddy dying and all."

I wanted to ask Gary Wayne how his daddy died, but my own folks had taught me better. So I said, "Chattahoochee, hey, that's real country."

He laughed. "The back forty, for sure. Gramma and Grandpa made me go to school and all. That's what got me in trouble."

"Going to school got you in trouble?"

"Sorta. I suppose some of the local boys decided they would like my motor scooter for their very own. So they took mine when I was in school. Then I took it back."

"That got you in trouble?"

"I sorta had to take it back by force, if you know what I mean. So they put me in jail."

"But it was yours, Gary Wayne. Why would they put you in jail for taking back your own property?"

"I ask myself that all the time. I suppose it had to do with what side of the constable's family those boys belonged."

"But that ain't right. No sir, not at all. Ain't right."

"You know the worst part?"

"What's that?"

"I still ain't got my motor scooter back."

I didn't know what to say to that. I wanted to tell Gary Wayne that all he had to do was get himself a lawyer, but that's when I remembered how it was that being under eighteen years of age, we didn't have the right to a lawyer, in those days. Still, jailing a fellow for taking back his own property did not sound fair to me. I asked him how long he had been in the reformatory.

"Year and a half."

Now I was scared. I had figured I would be put in the camp till the sheriff decided I wasn't lying. Once I got out, I could figure a way to help Hannah Jane. Listening to Gary Wayne, I wondered if I would ever get out.

On the first monthly visiting day, I posed the question to Daddy. We sat at the redwood picnic tables in what was called "the yard." It wasn't much of a yard, only about half the size of a football field, covered with dirt or mud, depending on the weather. It sat at a corner of the compound, cornered by the chain-link fence and the dormitory buildings where we lived.

Daddy wore his overalls, like usual. Momma had on her flowered church-going dress. I felt a lump well up from my chest and tears come to my eyes when I saw her, because I knew she dressed nice just for me. Every now and then, Daddy snuck a peek at the chain-link fence and razor wire.

He wasn't comfortable there, but he tried to hide it when he talked. "Son, I can't get nothing out of that old man," Daddy said, referring to the sheriff.

"But I ain't lying, Daddy. I swear to you, I ain't."

Daddy had a helpless look on his face. "I'll be honest with you, Chester. Were you older, I could get you one of them court-appointed lawyers. But they tell me they're considering making you a permanent ward of the court. When I asked the social worker what that meant, she explained it so, I wished she hadn't."

"What are we gonna do, Daddy?" I asked, trying to keep from crying so Momma wouldn't start in again.

Daddy took a deep breath, which usually meant bad news. "I'm saving as much money as I can, son, but times ain't so good at the plant just now. So you just gonna have to be patient for a while."

Like a year and a half, I figured.

Momma cried when she and Daddy had to leave.

"Tell Aldous I miss him," I said. I turned and started to leave real quick because I was just about to cry for the first time since I'd been there. But I made myself turn back anyway and said, "Momma, Daddy, I love you. I'm gonna be okay, I promise." Then I hugged them and couldn't hold back my tears. They cried too. All three of us, closer than I guess we'd ever been before, just cried and didn't care who saw us.

That night, lying there in that cold dormitory, I felt warm inside. It didn't matter so much for a while, being locked up there like that. I felt the nearness of my parents, and some of my confidence returned. *It will all work out,* I assured myself.

Next day, I wound up back in the hole.

CHAPTER THIRTEEN

There's a time for running
And a time for funning and
A time to take a stand.

I LOOKED STRAIGHT into Gary Wayne's eyes and saw a killer. He was out to get me, and I wanted to know why.

"Why, Gary Wayne, why you doing this to me?"

He didn't bat an eye. "'Cause I'm tired being nice to you!"

My heart sank. I knew what was coming.

"Checkmate!" he said. Third time in less than an hour.

"No fair," I said.

"Yeah, fair," he said. "You never going to learn to play this game if'n I keep going easy on you."

He was right, and I knew it. We sat at one of the wooden picnic tables in the yard, our prison-issue dungaree jackets pulled up tight against the cold, playing a game I was learning how to lose. My folks had sent me a for-real plastic chess game for my birthday. Gary Wayne had just begun to set up the pieces for the next game, when I saw them coming.

Joe Ray. Seven others. Big as him. They ambled across the yard in our direction. Since there was no one else around, my guess was, they intended to visit us.

"Maybe you oughta go somewhere," I said to Gary Wayne, looking past him over his left shoulder. "Looks like I got some business to attend to."

"Let's play chess," he said. Gary Wayne looked as unconcerned as I was concerned.

"Somehow, I don't think we'll finish the game, Gary Wayne."

"Your move," he said.

"Gary Wayne, I'm not sure what I should be doing just now. But I don't guess it's making a chess move."

I saw the same look in his eyes he had just before his queen slammed my king. He said, "Ain't nothing in life worthwhile is free or easy. Sometimes, you just can't run from a fight, 'cause it's gonna follow you till you stand up to it."

I hadn't planned to run. Only, it came to me that I fairly expected to pay the price for that. The look in Gary Wayne's face did not seem to share my fear. I took a deep breath and said, "Didn't you ever lose a fight?"

He smiled. "Lost lots of them. Lost at chess too, but I still play the game."

By that time, Joe Ray and the other boys had circled us. Joe Ray bent over and took my knight off the board.

"Hey, lookee here." He held the black piece up for the other boys to see. "These-here girls still play with dolls."

The other boys laughed, like they were expected to do. Then Joe Ray reached for one of Gary Wayne's pieces, but before he could get it, Gary Wayne took hold of it in his hand. Joe Ray's grin turned sour. He reached out his hand, palm up, expecting Gary Wayne to give him the chess piece. Gary Wayne looked at Joe Ray's hand and snorted up a fair ball of snot. I never doubted what he was about to do with it.

I stood just in time, looked up at Joe Ray's face, and said, "That chess piece is mine. Give it back!"

I didn't scare him, but I did distract him.

He stood a good seven or eight inches taller than me and had me by twenty, maybe thirty, pounds. I began to regret what I said to him, when he laughed in my face. "Baby Chester wants his doll back," he said.

"Yeah," the others aped, "Baby Chester wants his doll back."

Joe Ray held out his fist in front of me. I almost choked on his breath. He still hadn't discovered the purpose of a toothbrush.

"Watch this," he said to the other boys. He opened his hand, holding the knight directly under my nose. "Here, Baby Chester, take your ole doll back."

I already knew what he planned to do, but I reached for the piece anyway. He pulled it away, then slapped me in the face with his other hand. That part, I hadn't expected.

Tears rushed from my eyes, like someone had primed a pump. There was no way I could stop them, but I tried.

Joe Ray laughed again. "Look! Baby Chester's crying. Poor Baby Chester." He slapped me again.

The others laughed, this time on their own, with no prompting from Joe Ray. They found something to distract them from the boredom of prison life: me. The more they laughed, the more the tears ran down my face. He slapped me again. They laughed some more. I cried some more.

But this time, the more I cried, the madder I got. Joe Ray laughed louder, slapped me again, then threw his head back and let out a guffaw I was sure could be heard all the way back to Transylvania County.

That's when I hit him.

Sounded like a firecracker. *Kapooowww*. Smack across that extended, smart-aleck, guffawing jaw, sticking out there, pretty as a slow pitch over the center of the plate in softball. I don't remember doing it, but I hit him. I know I did, because next thing I knew, his guffaw sounded more like an *uuuuughhh*.

He crumpled to his knees. All of a sudden, considerably shorter than me. I started to remember the details of what happened clearly from that point on.

I know because it struck me: *Hey, he's shorter than me now.* So I hit him again, and again. He got shorter each time.

When I looked around, Gary Wayne was all arms and legs and fists, swinging like a wild animal cornered by a bear. Before long, we stood there back to back, swinging at whoever got close.

Didn't last long, the fight didn't.

Joe Ray lay on the ground, bleeding from the nose and moaning about how much it hurt. The other boys left as soon as they discovered the game wasn't fun anymore. No one bothered to try to pick up Joe Ray.

A handful of officers arrived to take the three of us to the hole. It was the second time Gary Wayne and I were to be locked up like that—and the last.

CHAPTER FOURTEEN

Jailbird, jailbird,
Caged and asking why.
Jailbird, jailbird,
Wings were meant to fly.

"I'M GETTING OUT OF HERE," Gary Wayne said.

We occupied our isolation cell and were in the process of figuring out a new use for toilet paper. He decided to warm up leftover soup by burning the tissue roll from the inside out, using the steel soup bowl to regulate the oxygen feeding the flames. He used up most of the kitchen matches hidden in the hollowed-out sole of his shoe before we got the makeshift campfire going right.

"What did you say, Gary Wayne?"

"I said, I'm getting out of this place. Gonna run for it."

I argued with him. "Why? You ain't done nothing wrong. They're gonna let you out—"

"They? You got any idea who 'they' are?" He waited for me to answer.

"Okay, no," I finally said, "but it just don't seem fair that—"

"That's why I got to do it myself. Ain't no 'they' out there. Nobody gonna help me. My momma can't do squat. Besides, I aim to get my motor scooter back. One way to do that, you know. I'm getting out of here."

He convinced me. Fact is, he made his argument so persuasively, I decided it must have applied to me as well. So I said, "Me too!"

Soon as I said it, I remembered the last time I'd said "Me too!" I wondered about Hannah Jane. I wondered if anyone would ever believe me. There had been days when I could forget about her. Days like the business with Joe Ray that got Gary Wayne and me in the hole. Never nights, though. Nights, I could see it all again in my mind.

I could hear Hannah Jane scream, could see the aliens clear as glass—as indeed they almost seemed to be. Yes, I wanted to escape, to fly away from that place. Not only for the freedom of it. I had a place to go, a place I feared almost as much as I needed to revisit. Gary Wayne had other ideas.

"I can't let you go with me," he said. "Too dangerous. You'll be out of here before long, anyway."

I disagreed loudly. "I got to go with you! They're never going to let me out of here."

Gary Wayne had never asked me why I was in the reformatory. Even if *I* hadn't followed those unwritten rules, *he* had. I wanted to tell him why I had to escape with him, but I knew if I did, he wouldn't let me go, for sure. Still, I had no choice. I had to trust that our friendship would survive my honesty.

"Look," I said, "I'm in here because . . . well, I suppose you ought to know . . . I could be charged with two murders I didn't commit."

Gary Wayne tried to look as if it didn't matter to him what I did or didn't do. But I could tell by the way his eyes widened, it mattered.

"I said, I didn't do it, Gary Wayne."

He said, "Ain't my business to judge no one."

"Problem isn't only whether I did it or not. Problem is, they're still alive, more or less. The problem is, they're not dead. Those people I'm accused of killing are not dead. Course, unless I find a way to help them, they may as well be."

I caught his attention, which didn't surprise me, because by the time I finished, my voice had stretched so high I almost screamed. If Gary Wayne didn't want to listen, at least he would hear me.

But he did listen.

"Hey, ease up," he said. "Now, why don't you tell me what this is all about."

I did. It took a while. But I told him. And he heard me. By the time that night was over, he agreed to take me with him.

I can't say he actually believed me. Gary Wayne was no fool. All the same, he agreed to take me with him.

He had a plan.

Took him a year to figure it out.

But it could work.

We started on it the day we got out of the hole.

The first part of the plan, according to Gary Wayne, involved getting access to a tool that could cut through heavy-gauge wire. I guessed correctly he meant the same gauge as the wire fence surrounding the camp.

Gary Wayne said, "That means you gotta get in good with the warden."

I caught the warden in the yard, admiring his rhododendron bushes. "Mr. Boss," I said. He liked being called "Boss," even though his real name was Pendergrast. "Mr. Boss, you need help with that garden over there?" I pointed to the greenhouse, where he kept his perennials and potted houseplants.

He smiled, still not friendly, but I did touch him where he seemed most vulnerable. "What kind of trouble you looking to get into now, Crazy Chester?" He called me the name I earned beating up on Joe Ray.

"I ain't looking to get into trouble, Mr. Boss. Most like, stay out of it."

He squeezed his face even tighter than it was and said, "What does my greenhouse have to do with you staying out of trouble?"

I told him the story I had made up, with the help of Gary Wayne: "Well, sir, back home I used to be in charge of our flower garden. I kinda thought if I did something I liked to do, I could keep busy and out of trouble. Like the preacher always says, an idle mind is the devil's . . . the devil's. . . ."

"Workshop." He finished my sentence, like I hoped he would. He scratched the white whiskers on his chin. "Just what you have in mind?"

"Mr. Boss, I sure would like to work in that greenhouse of yours. It would be good for me and for them plants that need all the attention a fellow can give them."

He smiled, friendly-like for the first time, and said, "I'll just have to give that some thought."

I started the next morning. The first part of our escape plan worked. Working in the warden's greenhouse, I had a job that allowed me access to tools. We still hadn't figured out how to justify my using the bolt cutters we would need to cut through the fence. But it was a start.

It wasn't till after lights out one night a few weeks later that I found out the other details of the plan. About two in the morning, Gary Wayne woke me. "Meet me in the jigs," he whispered. I don't know why, but in that place, the toilet was called "the jigs." He looked around to make sure everyone else was asleep, then crept barefoot into the outhouse connected to the dorm.

The housing officer snored assuringly. All I could see were the soles of his feet, propped up on the Army surplus metal desk in the chicken-wire cage that separated him from us. I waited a few minutes, then went into the narrow wooden toilet, a ten holer fitted with pine boards, now worn smooth from years of use. Because of the odor, the jigs remained open at the top. When it rained or snowed, most of us risked constipation to avoid sitting down out there. But just now, the jigs became an important part of our escape plan.

Gary Wayne stood up on the top of the boards, carefully straddling one of the holes. "Look here," he whispered.

I got up there next to him and peeked through a crack between two planks. That's when it hit me, full force. I said, "Holy smoke, Gary Wayne, you sure all this is necessary? There are some smells a body just don't want to get used to."

"Shhh." He hushed me, ignoring my complaint. "You just watch and wait. Gonna see something interesting."

It wasn't long before we heard the sputter of the perimeter pickup truck rounding the corner of the dirt road surrounding the chain-link fence.

"Now, you start counting the minutes," Gary Wayne said. "Soon as they pass by here, you count. See how long it takes before they drive by here again. Pay attention, now. Don't you let your mind go to wandering. This is gonna be right important if we're gonna make good our escape."

One thousand one, one thousand two, one thousand three. Through cracks in the planking, I made out the two officers, sitting in the slow-moving, powder-blue, '52 Chevy pickup truck. *One thousand four, one thousand five, one thousand six.* The man in the passenger seat held a double-barrel shotgun beside him, its barrel pointed at an angle out the open window. The driver shined a spotlight as the truck passed by the fence across the yard from our latrine. *One thousand seven, one thousand eight, one thousand nine.* He spotted the light up and down the fence and inside the yard. Finding nothing out of the ordinary, they drove on, the rickety pickup rattling from the washboard road.

Now and then, Gary Wayne poked a finger in my side to keep my mind focused. Nothing else to do, I kept on counting, determined to estimate the minutes best I could. I reached thirty. No truck yet. By about thirty-five minutes of my estimate, they came by again.

"Now, do it again," Gary Wayne instructed me, allowing I had come close to the actual thirty minutes around which, by his own estimate, the perimeter officers scheduled their rounds. I did, this time slowing down a bit. Thirty-two minutes before they passed again.

"Do it again," Gary Wayne said.

The look I gave him was not very compliant.

"Do it again," he repeated. "You'll figure it out soon enough. I did."

But this time, when I reached thirty-nine minutes, they still hadn't come by. He kept poking me with his finger, saying, "Keep counting."

Forty-five minutes. Nothing. Finally, at about sixty-seven minutes, the truck clattered around the corner, flashed its spotlight, and went on.

"I don't get it, Gary Wayne."

He said, "It's after three in the morning. They stretch out their security rounds after three. Reckon they figure no one'll try to get through that fence by then. But the real reason, I suppose, is they get sleepy, so by now they're probably bagging it in that old pickup truck."

In the morning, after breakfast, he explained how his escape plan came to him: "I learned it from a rabbit," he said.

"A rabbit," I said. "You learned your escape plan from a rabbit?"

He smiled like he did when he was about to make a clever move in chess. "One night when I was leaning up against the jigs wall, taking care of business, I looked between the boards and saw the perimeter truck pass by the fence. They spotlighted the yard, then went on about their rounds. That's when I saw it."

"The rabbit?"

"That's right, the rabbit. It comes outta the woods there, scoots under the fence, hops on over to the back of the mess hall, and commences to rummage through the trash pile dumped out there every night for the early morning crew. I watched Mr. Rabbit play around in that trash heap for a while, 'cause I got nothing else to do.

"All of a sudden, it scampers back to the fence, scoots under, and hops back to the woods. Less than a minute passes, and the perimeter truck comes by. Soon as it passes, the rabbit comes out the woods, back into the yard, and resumes its rummaging. It's around two-thirty in the morning. I watch ole Mr. Rabbit time that truck again. Thirty minutes, he hightails it, then returns following the perimeter truck.

"I figure, he's got it all timed. The next time, though, he doesn't cut out like I think he will. I'm thinking, maybe he's confused, so I wait to see him scamper when he gets surprised by the spotlight from the truck. But it don't happen."

By then, even I had figured out the end of the rabbit story. "He took off in an hour, instead of thirty minutes," I said, proud of my deductive abilities.

"That's right," Gary Wayne said. "Ole Mr. Rabbit had them boys figured."

I said, "That's your plan, isn't it? We wait till the perimeter officers take their three o'clock nap, cut the fence, and scamper out of here like that rabbit."

Gary Wayne smiled.

I smiled too, but there was something about the rabbit story that still pestered me. "By the way, Gary Wayne, what happened to Mr. Rabbit? I didn't see him out there last night."

Gary Wayne stopped smiling. "Nothing in life is certain, Chess," he said. "One night, them boys in that truck came by earlier than usual, spotted their light on Mr. Rabbit, and filled his poor hide with buckshot. Ooooh, ooooh, you shoulda seen the boys haul their collective butts outta their cots."

Gary Wayne didn't miss the look on my face. "Hey, Chess," he said, "it's the best plan I got. I do believe the officers in that truck are lazy. It's a gamble, and I reckon we're not in a position to up and walk out the front gate. So we may as well give it a try."

The warden was suspicious. "What you got there in your hands, Chester?" He stopped me in the yard, halfway between the maintenance building and the greenhouse.

I tried to act stupid. "In my hands?" I said, followed by, "Sure is a nice day, ain't it, Mr. Boss?"

He would not be distracted. "I said, what's that you got in your hands, Chester?"

"Shears." I bent the truth a mite. They were bolt cutters I had requisitioned from the tool shop, telling the officer in charge that the warden wanted me to use them to trim his rhododendron bushes.

"Don't look like shears to me."

"Well, Mr. Boss, I reckon they ain't exactly shears, but they do work to trim the rhododendron bushes out there in front of your office."

He squinched his face up like he did when he was thinking. "Where'd you get them?"

"I requisitioned them from the tool shop. Told Officer Potts exactly what they were for. He said, 'That's good, Chester, 'cause the warden there has some of the finest rhododendron bushes in this-here county. But heaven knows, they do need a little trimming back, now and then.'"

Warden Pendergrast looked over at his office and rubbed his chin. He turned his head sideways, first to the right, then the left. "Okay," he said, "just make sure you use them on the bushes."

I did. By the time we were ready to make a break for it, the warden's rhododendron bushes looked considerably smaller than when I started pruning them. Nobody even questioned me or saw anything out of the ordinary when I walked around with those bolt cutters, along with the other gardening tools. Like Gary Wayne said, there's always exceptions to the rules, so long as they suit the warden.

It was getting on late winter when we decided to go for it. And, as I was about to discover, none too soon. A new prisoner had been seen walking across the yard to do his rules in the tiny brick schoolhouse. They said he was tall and good-looking and had eyes that got your attention, and it seemed awful funny that he made a point of asking one of the boys if he knew me.

He asked a young prisoner named Chris, who had been sent to the reformatory together with his brother, Teddy. The two of them kind of stood out because they were smart enough to stay out of trouble, and clever enough to provide information to the other boys for favors, like extra desserts and such. That's why I took it seriously when Chris said to me, "Tall kid asked for you. Said your name as if he had known you all your life."

"Yeah, that's so," Teddy said, "just like he'd known you all his life."

I never knew how it was the two of them had managed to get themselves into jail like that, but I did not doubt the veracity of their information. There are some folks in prison who just seem to know what's going on. Someone had come looking for me. Someone— who, by reliable description, could be the spitting image of John Croshaw—now sat in a schoolroom, copying out a book of rules.

How he managed to get himself into the reformatory, I did not know. Nor did I make plans to find out. That night, we would make a run for it. Of that, I had no doubt.

CHAPTER FIFTEEN

The best-laid plans of mice and men
Can fail you when you're in the pen.

WE HAD JUST REACHED the perimeter fence, when we heard the pickup truck clatter in our direction. I never thought I could jump so high. Both of us landed back in the jigs in time to watch the two officers shine their lights on the yard. One of them cursed, then said to the other, "I think ole Ralph's seeing things tonight." He got on the truck radio, and we heard him say, "There ain't nothing out here. You seeing things again, Ralph?"

Across the compound, at the far corner from where we were, a twenty-foot tower guarded the front entrance. It was put there to open and close the main gate, allowing traffic in and out of the compound. The tower officer could see only the top of the fence we planned to cut through. The dormitory building covered us, so long as we stayed low.

What we hadn't considered was that to get to the fence, we had to cross an opening between the dormitories and the rest of the compound. It wasn't much of an opening, but if the tower officer was looking in that direction, he could make out movement even if he couldn't see us clearly.

Gary Wayne wasn't daunted. "That's okay," he said. "Next time, we crawl across the yard."

"When's next time, Gary Wayne?" I asked, thinking that maybe "next time" might not be such a good idea and that maybe we should wait a few weeks and think about it some more. Then I thought of John Croshaw. "Okay, Gary Wayne," I said, "when do we try again?"

"In about an hour, after the truck passes by again."

At least, I didn't have much time to fret about it. But I started worrying when the truck passed by in half an hour instead of the full hour we had estimated. It occurred to me that maybe the boy in the schoolhouse wasn't John Croshaw, after all. I said to Gary Wayne, "Guess they're a little spooked. Maybe we ought to try—"

"Tonight's the night, Chess." He cut me off. "You don't have to go with me, but I may not be able to work up enough courage to try again. There's no moon and plenty of cloud cover. I won't hold it against you if you decide not to go."

I guess that was the first time I discovered Gary Wayne was as human and scared as I was. He just kept it to himself better. "Let's do it!" I said.

We waited till the truck passed and we couldn't hear it clunking and rattling anymore. Then we shinnied over the latrine wall for the second time that night. We crept across the compound till we reached the opening between the dormitories.

"Down on our bellies," Gary Wayne said.

I carried the bolt cutters, and he dragged along a gunnysack full of food and other stuff we would need once we cleared the fence. It took us a few minutes. It seemed an hour. The whole time, we listened for the perimeter truck. I tried not to imagine how I would look with buckshot in my hide. By the time we made it to the fence, I estimated we had about twenty minutes to cut through the wire and cross the outer perimeter, which was in clear view of the front gate tower. We would have to crawl across that, too.

So far, nothing had gone the way we'd planned it. As we worked on the fence, I wondered what else would go wrong.

"This is harder than I thought," I said to Gary Wayne. I struggled to cut through the wire links.

"We'll work in shifts," he said. "Just keep low."

In a few minutes, I had cut a section only half big enough for us to squeeze through. "Your turn," I said. The muscles of my hands were worn out. It would have been easy enough, had we been able to dig under the fence. But the builders had figured that one out. A deep concrete footer had been laid along the fence line to prevent anyone from tunneling under.

Gary Wayne was almost through the fence. By every calculation, even if the truck came every thirty minutes from there on, we still had about five minutes to crawl across the perimeter road and run for it through the woods. That was calling it close, but Gary Wayne was optimistic.

"Given the level of their intelligence," he said, "it should take them an hour to figure out who's run and another to get themselves together for the hunt. We should have a two-hour head start—even more, if the warden decides to take over."

We started to squeeze through the fence, dragging the bolt cutter and gunnysack. Gary Wayne stopped to push the wire back in place, on the off chance the perimeter officers would miss the holes in it. We saw the spotlight before we heard the truck. They were early. Those boys were nervous—and had every reason to be.

We didn't crawl. We ran, barely making it across the thirty-yard outer perimeter clearing, when the truck stopped at the fence. We threw ourselves down into the ground fern at the base of the woods just in time to avoid being picked up by the spotlight. Gary Wayne put his finger to his lips, signaling me to keep quiet.

The perimeter officers aimed the spotlight along the edge of the woods. We kept our heads down. I heard them talking. They didn't seem too happy about the situation. "We got a problem here," one of them said on the radio. He listened for orders. The radio crackled. Then I heard the perimeter officer say, "Tracks? No, we ain't looked for no tracks yet."

That was our signal to take off. Our trail had already been laid. Officers kept the fence perimeter cut and free of any kind of vegetation. Regularly, they raked the dirt smooth so anyone stepping across the road would leave tracks clear enough to follow into the woods. That way, they could set their dogs on the scent, and the search would begin on the right trail.

At the time, we didn't concern ourselves much with the problems of the perimeter officers. We ran for about ten minutes, dodging trees and underbrush, trying to put as much distance between us and the camp as possible. When we reached a small creek, Gary Wayne signaled for me to stop.

"It will take a while," he said, "but by first light, the dogs will be on our scent."

"We gonna follow the creek?" I asked, thinking that would cover our scent from the dogs.

"No," Gary Wayne said. "Dogs follow a smell from your body, as well as your feet. When they go after us, they'll sniff the air as much as the ground. So we best take off all our clothes, right now."

I said, "Gary Wayne, I'm not all that modest, but don't you think we'll get cold out here without clothes?"

"We got clothes," he said, pulling what looked to be dirty laundry out of the gunnysack he carried.

I almost passed out from the odor. "Gary Wayne, those clothes smell almost bad as Joe Ray." He smiled, and I got it. I said, "Those are Joe Ray's clothes, right?"

Gary Wayne nodded. "I got them from the laundry room when he turned in his dirty clothes last week, after wearing them a few months or so. Here's what we gonna do."

He explained that the dogs would be introduced to our scent by letting them sniff something personal, like our spare clothes or bedding on our bunks. Once they had our scent, they could pick it up from where we crawled through the fence. From there, they'd follow it as far as it took them. Any other scent would be ignored unless given directly to the dogs by their handlers.

"Help me out here." Gary Wayne bundled together some broken tree limbs and tied our clothes to the makeshift raft with string he had unraveled from the gunnysack. He launched the whole lot into the stream. "Let's hope they have a nice long ride. Maybe it'll confuse them for a while."

I thought I would pass out, wearing Joe Ray's dirty clothes.

"Just think of it as the smell of freedom," Gary Wayne said.

"Gary Wayne, freedom never smelled like this."

We headed into the deep woods. It was the second time I had dared to do something I probably shouldn't have done. I felt as if I were sinking into a hole that kept getting deeper and deeper. I knew if I couldn't find a way to free Hannah Jane and maybe some of the other kidnapped children, I would never get out of my own personal prison. I had added "escaped prisoner" to my list of crimes, which included kidnapping and maybe murder. All I had to rely on? A friend no better off than me and whose one goal in life was to retrieve a motor scooter.

I thought, *It can't get worse.* But something in my stomach said, *Are you sure of that?*

For it had suddenly hit me: What if John Croshaw had been arrested and admitted his part in Hannah Jane's kidnapping, and what if he had told the authorities of my innocence, and what if they had intended to release me in the morning. . . .

CHAPTER SIXTEEN

From woods deep, dark
I hear the bark
Of dogs or maybe wolves.
And on this night
Of pale moonlight,
The deer take to their hooves.

BY THE SECOND NIGHT OUT, we had eaten all our food. Our clothes no longer smelled bad, or maybe we just couldn't smell anymore. It was about five in the morning. We were asleep under a fallen bitternut hickory log when I heard the dogs baying. Gary Wayne woke as fast as I did.

"Looks like they picked up our scent again," he said. "Let's get a move on."

We headed away from the sound of the dogs, best we could.

"How far you reckon they are, Gary Wayne?"

"Can't say for sure." He stopped to listen. "I'd say three, maybe five miles. Sound carries a long way up here in these mountains. We best put as much distance between them and us as we can."

In an hour, the dogs had gained on us. Gary Wayne picked up a tree limb and trimmed it, using the bolt cutters we took with us after we made it through the perimeter fence.

I asked him, "You're not planning to fight them dogs with that stick, are you?"

"It's for bear," he said. He didn't look like he was joking.

"Gary Wayne, bears are the least of our concerns right now." I couldn't understand why he would worry at all, since everyone knew the bears wouldn't be out of their dens for another month or so.

Gary Wayne enlightened me. "I'm not trying to avoid them, Chess, I'm a-fixing to find me one." He was getting used to the questioning looks on my face, so I didn't have to ask him to explain.

"We need to give the dogs something they like to chase even more than us."

I was beginning to appreciate Gary Wayne. His plan had worked so far, more or less. There was no reason to suspect he was crazy. I just hoped the bear we were after knew that.

To be helpful, I asked, "What should we be looking for? They don't hang out a 'Do not disturb' sign, now, do they?"

"In a way," he said, "there are signs. Plenty of signs. My grampa showed me all the time, always taking me out to the woods where he showed me the wild creatures and their wild ways. So we look for their signs now."

"Like what, Gary Wayne?"

"Like dug-up yellow-jacket or ant nests, overturned logs and rocks, broken or twisted branches. Black bears usually den up high, here in these mountains, up big old dead trees. You can look for squawroot near the root of trees; they hanker for squawroot. . . ."

As we walked, he told me about more signs. Some I knew, others I'd never heard of. But, looking back, I had seen every one of them on hikes through the woods with my daddy. Daddy never feared bear. Still, he had rules I was to follow strictly:

"Never abuse an animal in the wild, Chester. He was here before you and me, so it's his home. You wouldn't go walking into someone's house, cutting down their furniture, now, would you?"

Daddy was right about that.

"They are timid creatures who hide from man," he continued. "But being bashful don't mean they're afraid."

Daddy once told me a story about how not to treat a bear. "One old bear ate a logger out here not too long ago," he warned me. "Man lived in an old logging cabin. Trashed out his camp something awful. Got tired of a big old bear eating around his cabin, so instead of cleaning up the place, he shot the bear. Gut-shot him, worst possible place to try to kill a bear. The wounded bear got so mad he tore down the man's door and killed him. Both died, Chess. Neither one had to."

"Over there!" Gary Wayne pointed to a marshy depression with thick vegetation. "Carolina cove," he said. "Bears favor them for the berries and other plants they like to eat in the summer and fall. See how torn up the bushes are? Some bear's staked out this territory for his very own."

He craned his neck toward the trees. "Look for a hole in the tree trunks, Chess." They were oak, maple, beech—trees of the Carolina hardwood forests. "Older trees," Gary Wayne said. "Look for the older, dead ones."

That's when I saw it.

Remarkable, I thought, how you can see something when you have half an idea what you're looking for. I saw it because the bark had been stripped around what I was sure was a hole. At first, I almost gave it up for being too small. But I remembered Gary Wayne had said, "Hole's not big, foot and a half, no more. You wouldn't believe what bears can crawl into."

I said to Gary Wayne, "Don't suppose a bear could crawl into that opening, do you?" I pointed about thirty feet up a birch tree.

He smiled and said, "I reckon one could."

It took Gary Wayne only a few seconds to shinny up the tree, using the knobs of broken branches and an initial boost from me. I happily forsook the honor of seeing if my perception was fruitful. When he got to the top, he pulled himself up to the hole and peeked in, like a kid looking for cookies. He looked down at me and smiled.

"What's he doing?" I asked.

"Looking at me," he answered.

All of a sudden, I heard a wolfing and blowing sound coming from the tree den. It didn't take much time at all for Gary Wayne to shinny down that tree.

"What do we do now?" I said.

"I guess we wait."

It was about eight in the morning. Neither one of us expressed a desire for breakfast. The baying of the dogs kept sounding closer. Gary Wayne estimated their position no more than a mile from us. "Oughta take an hour or more through that thicket," he said. "Let's make sure them hound dogs come right on up to this tree." He laughed like he had mischief in mind. "Follow me, Chess."

We went back down the trail, retracing our steps from the day before. Gary Wayne stopped at an old-growth hickory, unbuttoned his striped convict trousers, and peed on the tree. I got the idea, found myself a likely target, and let fly.

"Don't use it up all at once," said Gary Wayne.

I said, "Don't worry, I get the picture."

We got so carried away with marking our scent and such that we almost peed ourselves into trouble.

I concentrated on forcing out the last drops of what I had in reserve, when I peed on the nose of the lead hound dog. She had been sniffing right along, a ways up ahead of the others, probably their best trail dog. I had taken dead aim at a fallen maple log when she trotted out into the clearing I shared with Gary Wayne. The hound dog and I both stopped what we were doing and stared at one another. I was embarrassed, but that all went away when she commenced to baying like she had found what it was she was looking for—which she had.

We couldn't help ourselves for laughing. Gary Wayne and I hooted our lungs out, trying to get our equipment back in our trousers, with that hound dog baying and the others less than a hundred yards behind with their handlers. Gary Wayne went over to the old dog and patted her on the head. Then we took off with her on our heels. We kept laughing all the way back to the bear-occupied birch tree.

"You ready?" I said to Gary Wayne, who was now climbing back up the birch tree. The dogs' baying sounded no more than a few yards away.

Gary Wayne had reached a position just below the bear's den. I heard the wolfing and coughing again as the bear expressed his discomfort with Gary Wayne's intrusion.

"Throw it to me," he said.

I took hold of a broken tree branch and launched it toward Gary Wayne. Not close enough.

The dogs were just about to our clearing.

"Try again." His voice sounded urgent this time.

I missed; the branch flew by, just out of his reach.

I looked back toward the sound of the dogs. The voices of men came back to me. Excited they were, the way a body sounds when he's about to close the trap.

"Chess, you just relax, now, and toss that branch like you would for the fun of it."

This time, the branch floated just above Gary Wayne's head and seemed to glide into his outreached hand. We had seconds to spare.

Dogs howled. Men hollered. Gary Wayne waited, his stick ready to jab into that hole, soon as they came into view.

Me, I fretted, undecided which would be worse: the hunting party and dogs who had chased us, fatefully it seemed, all the way up to this tree, or the bear who was going to chase us away from it.

"Get ready!" Gary Wayne said. "I see them down the trail."

What he saw, I heard. Dogs, men, and now—he started jabbing the stick into the hole—bear.

The creature let out a squeal, then a roar. The den seemed to come apart all at once as angry bits and pieces of black bear and bark began to fly in all directions. That bear did not suffer the interruption of his sleep lightly. First Gary Wayne, then the bear headed down the tree, directly at me.

Soon as Gary Wayne's feet hit the ground, we were off down the trail away from the searchers. Soon as the bear's paws hit the ground, he was off down the trail, breathing down our necks, howling and roaring and barking and growling with every step we took. The men screamed orders to the dogs, but the hounds were off after the bear. Just like we wanted.

Unfortunately, the bear did not seem to flash onto that fact just then.

I could barely talk, from panting, but I managed to point that out to Gary Wayne. "You do know that bear and them dogs are following us, don't you."

"Yes," he panted back. "But the bear's going down there." He pointed to another Carolina cove just ahead and down from where we were headed. "Bears dive into those marshy places when dogs are after them. Gives them lots of places to hide, and the dogs sink into the wet ground. That old bear ain't gonna get caught so easily, but them dogs are going to be distracted till some time the middle of the summer."

I said, "You hope."

Gary Wayne panted back, "I hope."

Just about the time I had given myself up for a goner, the fracas behind us took another turn. I could hear the men screaming, trying to get their dogs' attention. I could hear that old bear still making a fuss, but the sound faded with every yard we put between ourselves and them.

Gary Wayne knew bears and dogs. He knew their ways, how they acted when faced with this or that distraction, where they would go when chased, and which prey they preferred. He understood where that bear would go and how the dogs would go there in chase with the taste of the hunt in their mouths.

Yes, he knew for a-certain where they would go. But he knew nothing for sure of our present direction.

Neither one of us knew where we were going. By nightfall we

listened. Sat on our backsides and listened for signs of the dogs or men who had been following us. Nothing. Only the sounds of the woods. Reassuring sounds of nature at its peaceful best.

That didn't last long. For though it was clear we had lost the dogs, we found ourselves looking over our shoulders as we hiked.

"Did you see something?" Gary Wayne asked.

"No," I lied. I did indeed see something. Or maybe I sensed a presence. A flicker here, a shadow there. Once, I pulled up when I was sure I caught the outline of someone behind us.

"You *did* see someone," Gary Wayne said.

I did not answer.

Our hunger caught up with us. Sleep did nothing to ease the pain. By morning, I said the obvious: "We got to find something to eat, don't you think?"

He ignored my complaint, his feet making exhausting progress, with me lagging farther back with each step. Then he stopped, waited for me to catch up. I followed his finger across a shallow cove and up the side of a hill. "Lookee yonder, Chess. I do suppose there's food to be had. Course, I don't imagine it'll be free for the asking."

The cabin nestled up against a bank of birch and maple.

I looked at Gary Wayne. "I'm getting hungry enough to chance it. You don't suppose we might want to go on over there and pay our respects?"

He shrugged his shoulders. "I don't know, Chess. These mountain folk don't get many visitors."

"That's 'cause they shoot most of them, right?" I laughed.

The sound died in my throat when I heard the click of two hammers. I knew from experience with Daddy's guns. Someone had cocked a double-barrel shotgun.

The voice we heard sounded gravelly and firm. "That's right, young sir, we do shoot most of them. Now, reach."

We reached.

"You can just turn around real slow now, so as I can see who I got here."

Four arms to heaven, Gary Wayne and I turned around, like the man said, very slowly.

CHAPTER SEVENTEEN

Things are seldom what they seem.
Close you eyes, dream your dream.
Open up your heart and mind.
Oh, the treasures you might find.

THE FIRST TIME I caught sight of Owen Duffy, he held the barrels of his old twelve-gauge mere inches from our faces. I didn't get a good look at him, with the business end of that shotgun pointed at Gary Wayne and me.

"You boys must be lost, sure enough."

"Yes, sir," we said in unison.

The man turned out to be a quick judge of character, far as I was concerned. He dropped his shotgun to his side and walked past us. "Come along with me," he said. "You look hungry, well as lost."

We followed him toward the cabin. I took note of how his denim overalls hung loose on a body bent by the years, though still sure of step. He reminded me of most mountain men in those days. A faded flannel shirt kept his upper body warm. His high-top shoes showed signs of mending. He had pulled a woolen woodsman cap tight to his ears. I still hadn't seen his face, following him the way I was, but the back of his neck reminded me of a drought-cracked riverbed. He wore his hair short. The part of it I saw under the cap had turned pure white. I would have guessed the man to be in his late seventies. Eighty would not have surprised me.

As we crossed into the clearing of his cabin, he pulled up and turned toward his right. His raspy voice barked an order: "It's okay, Jule, you don't have to cover me no more."

A boy stepped out from behind an outhouse, set off a ways from the cabin. He cradled a J. C. Higgins single-shot .22 rifle. I thought he looked younger than Gary Wayne and me, not nearly old enough to be toting a firearm. But he did so with a look in his brown eyes that told me he knew well enough how to use it. His hair, cut like someone had laid a bowl on his head, hung straight above his shoulders. He had freckles across his nose and cheeks. The boy wore overalls, just like the old man.

"That there's Jule," the man said. "Knows how to use that firearm, case you're wondering."

Jule followed us into the cabin, still toting his rifle, a respectful, cautious distance from the two of us. I got the impression that even if the old man trusted us, Jule did not.

"Wash your hands before you take to the table." The man pointed to a wooden sink with a pump handle extended over it. I still couldn't see his face clearly inside the cabin, lighted as it was by a single coal-oil lantern resting on a table in the middle of the one and only room.

While Gary Wayne and I washed, Jule stirred the contents of an iron pot hanging over a wood fire in a moss-rock hearth that took up one whole side of the cabin. A hand-hewn cedar pole ladder led up to a loft, half the width of the bottom floor. I figured that would be Jule's place. An iron, single bed with a cotton tick mattress and coiled springs sat directly under the loft, off to the side of the fireplace. Two shuttered windows straddled the heavy, two-inch pine-plank front door, which locked with a heavy, wood bolt that could be drawn across the width of the door. The windows faced east.

Whoever had built the old cabin knew his business. Chinking between the peeled logs seemed to be a combination of mud and moss. Daddy, Aldous, and I had helped erect just such a cabin for a neighbor who decided to take up his residence in the woods. I knew from experience how well the chinking worked to keep out unwanted drafts.

The old man introduced himself. "Name's Owen P. Duffy." He didn't ask ours. Must have figured we had other things on our minds. "All we got is rabbit stew tonight. But I reckon you boys won't complain none."

We didn't. We couldn't get to the table fast enough. Gary Wayne and I pulled a plank bench out from one side of the table. Mr. Duffy and Jule took the other side. Jule had already prepared a large wooden bowl of stew, which sat there on the table, making my mouth water. We waited while Mr. Duffy and Jule bowed their heads to say their private prayers. The old man removed his hat, and it was then that I finally got a look at his face.

The wrinkles sat as deep as the ones on the back of his neck. He had a few threads of white hair atop his head, but it was the kind of head that wouldn't have looked right without being bald. When he opened his eyes after praying, they blinked hazel.

I thought of Momma Opalona and wondered if the two were related. Funny how a fellow can wonder fanciful things without making judgments.

The old man's white beard formed a goatee. I thought of a picture I had seen of Confederate General Pierre Gustave Toutant Beauregard. I added about ten years to my original estimate of his age. He was in his late eighties, if a day.

While we ate, nobody talked. Jule hadn't said a word since we first laid our eyes on him. I wondered if maybe the boy was a mute. But, at the time, conversation was the last thing that concerned me. My mind dwelt on my stomach, which truly relished the kernels of corn, pieces of potatoes, and cabbage that kept that poor rabbit company in the stew. Simple fare, for a-certain, but I would have said at the time, *food for kings.*

"Slow down!" Mr. Duffy instructed. "I can see you ain't eaten in a while. Y'all make yourselves sick, lessen you allows your stomachs to catch up with your appetites."

We slowed down. Not easy.

The old man looked us over. "When you finish eating, take off them convict clothes."

Gary Wayne and I looked at each other, not knowing what to make of the instruction, an obvious reference to our last place of residence.

Mr. Duffy continued, "Over that closet yonder"—he pointed to a pine chifforobe in a corner next to his cot—"there be clothing for you both. When you ready, bring me them uniforms."

I never asked what Mr. Duffy did with our striped wool trousers and shirts. That would be the first and last time he made mention of our previous accommodations. Apparently, none of his business. He did not judge us.

We finished supper and washed off the dishes under the hand pump in the wooden sink. We waited patiently for our hands to drip dry. Then we searched through the chifforobe for the fresh clothes Mr. Duffy had offered.

Gary Wayne had his convict pants halfway down his legs, when the man pointed to a wood frame dressing screen in the corner by the fireplace and said, "Son, have the decency not to drop your trousers in front of my granddaughter."

Gary Wayne looked over at Jule. The red came to his face faster than he ducked behind the screen. Jule was not a *he*, after all. The girl wore a shade of red almost as crimson as the one on Gary Wayne's face.

Not granddaughter. Great-granddaughter, actually. As we were to learn later from Mr. Duffy, her baptismal certificate said Julianne Marie Kelley. Like Gary Wayne, she was an orphan, the only child of Mr. Duffy's sole granddaughter. No one knew where her father had taken himself.

But his loss turned out to be our gain. We were to get to know Jule over the summer we spent on that mountain. Gary Wayne, especially.

Mr. Duffy woke us at five. We had slept out back in the tool shed. He made us an offer: "You boys earn your keep, you can stay with us, sleep in the shed, and eat all you want."

There was plenty of work to do. We looked like we'd been there all our lives, dressed as we were in patched overalls, compliments of the man who had taken us in. Mr. Duffy explained where the clothes came from and more.

"My own boys all passed away now. You can keep their old clothes. They moved on not long after their mother died." He looked up the hill from where we worked, ripping pine planks, and stripping logs with an ancient drawknife.

He didn't have to say anything else. We saw the picket fence and knew there would be graves sitting on that hill that faced the valley and the misty mountains beyond it. A single, mature sycamore shaded the mound.

Later, Jule told us that Mr. Duffy's sons had died at sea in the early days of World War II. He had placed the wooden grave markers to honor their lives. No bodies recovered. She said Mr. Duffy understood that to be the way of war.

And Jule's mother? She did lie up there on that peaceful hill. The death of her mother was another story that would give Gary Wayne and me an insight into the remarkable young woman we first took for a boy. But for now, we undertook the learning of a trade which also paid our room and board. Hard work did not describe it. Compared to the reformatory, the cutting and stripping and sawing of trees would come to rest in our bones like the pure feeling of freedom. And freedom was all that entertained our minds for the time being. I did not put much attention on Devil's Mountain, or trying to save Hannah Jane, or even on my current status as an escaped con. For now, I had food to eat, the warmth of a wooden shed, all the trees and mountains in the world in which to wander, and, maybe, some healing to do.

The time would come, I knew, when I would have to attend to other obligations. But now. . . .

Mr. Duffy promised, "You boys welcome to stay on long as you like. I can use the help just now. Pay is board and a few dollars a month, if you help me with the cabins." Mr. Duffy made log cabins. Built them by hand, as he had since he was a boy. "My own daddy taught me the trade," he explained. "When he wasn't gambling, that is. After the war, I took it up full time."

Even then, I had a passion for history, so I computed his estimated age and said, "After the Spanish-American War, sir?"

Mr. Duffy smiled. "I was too full of the evils of war to take part in that little demonstration."

That's when it hit me. I said, "Mr. Duffy, you were in the Civil War?" I thought I must be talking to a legend. My grandma used to tell me stories of her own daddy, who came out of the Civil War, migrated to Texas, and became a cowboy. But I never thought I would ever meet a real live Confederate veteran. Least, I assumed he was a Confederate veteran.

That part, I got right. I just couldn't wait to question him more. "Mr. Duffy, would you tell me about it?"

"The fight?"

"Yes, sir."

He chiseled away at a log with his adz, a tool almost no one had the skill to use anymore because it could take a good hunk out of your foot or leg if you failed to wield it true. He worked slowly, pacing himself, every movement of the tool kissing the timber at just the right angle. I thought he wouldn't answer.

Finally, he looked up at me. "What's your name, son?"

"Chester, sir."

"Well, Chester, you and your friend over there"—he pointed at Gary Wayne, who toted a sack of chicken feed while Jule tossed the grain to the clucking Rhode Island Reds mixing it up with one another over first rights to the feed—"you young'ns can wait till storytelling time in the evening, after supper, when we sit out on the porch and watch the sun drop down behind them blue mountains."

I was so excited the rest of the day, I worked extra hard just to keep from thinking about it.

We ate a lunch of warm bread, leftover rabbit stew, and early root vegetables from the garden. The patch lay downhill from the cabin, near a running stream dammed up from time to time to irrigate the crops when it didn't rain for a while.

Mr. Duffy took out his jackknife and cut a slice of long bread to dunk in the stew. He explained our task for the rest of the day: "We got to load some beams on the wagon, hitch it up to Lamech, and haul the lot down to the village."

I became distracted, recalling that Lamech, the father of Noah, lived seven hundred and seventy-seven years, which told me that Mr. Duffy's old mule really was an old mule. I wondered again about Mr. Duffy's age.

Gary Wayne interrupted my calculations when he asked, "What village, sir?"

Mr. Duffy said, "Balsam Grove."

That's when I knew Gary Wayne and I had been heading in the right direction.

Mr. Duffy must have noticed my reaction, because he said, "Got business down there, son?"

"Not in Balsam Grove, sir," I answered, leaving out the fact that it was only a few miles from my own home. He didn't ask any more questions.

Balsam Grove would take a two-hour drive down the mountain. Distance in the mountains is measured in time, not miles, since a three-mile trip can sometimes take twice as long as a six-mile one on flat ground. I had never been to the village before. I fretted some because I knew it lay in a part of Transylvania County where I risked being recognized.

I felt grateful to find the sawmill located outside the town proper, on the trail down which we had traveled.

Mr. Duffy must have noticed my nervousness, because he said, "You boys stay here and get ready to unload the wagon, whilst I go in there and settle up with the owner." He crossed the yard, strewn with feather-edged kindling, to a makeshift pine shack.

A man with an unkempt beard stepped out with Mr. Duffy, spit out a wad of brown, juicy tobacco, and pointed to a pile of beams next to a large gasoline-powered ripsaw. "You can stack them yonder," he said. They were hand-hewn beams, like Mr. Duffy's.

Earlier, on the way down to the village, Mr. Duffy had explained that some folks like their wood cut by hand because it made their homes look more "original." It was one of those grownup things, I decided, figuring one day I'd understand how something that looked so unfinished could be so valuable.

Mr. Duffy and the man shook on it. We unloaded the beams and headed Lamech back up the trail.

I hadn't seen any money change hands, and I let my curiosity get the better of me. "How much you get for a pile of wood like that, Mr. Duffy?"

He cocked his head and looked at storm clouds, moving across the cove up the trail a mile or so. "Gonna get rained on," he said.

I figured I had asked a personal question and felt embarrassed for being so nosy.

Mr. Duffy said, "Trade."

I looked at Gary Wayne, who didn't get it either. "Sir?" I said.

."Trade," he repeated. "He pays me in trade. Come fall, I ride back down and take home a wagonload of dry goods and supplies and fresh vegetables and apples and such, to put up for winter."

My mind flashed to the sandblasted root-cellar door just outside the back of Mr. Duffy's cabin. It was my first experience with a form of commerce called trade by some, barter by others.

Our clothes, rain-soaked and heavy, clung to our bodies by the time Lamech pulled the wagon into the clearing. We would have work to do before we could attend to the wet and cold that nagged at us. Our labor did not come without its rewards: the good feelings we found when we'd put in an honest day's work.

The smell of fresh dirt hung in the air. Rebirth, I thought, the land washed clean by the shower that seemed to touch the soul of the earth and the creatures that lived upon it.

As we unharnessed Lamech, a dark cloud slipped over the mountain, chasing a cold, gusty wind and sending the debris of the woods in front of it. I lowered my head to the wind, determined to finish my chores before I would enjoy the warmth of the cabin. The darkness of the storm took over. A bolt of lightning flashed against the hill above us. We rushed Lamech into his stall and started for the safety of our cabin. Darker now, a fearsome dark. Another flash of lightning, and I pulled up, my gaze lifted to the black ridge above the cabin. I waited, the rain cutting directly into my eyes.

Gary Wayne called out, "This way, you crazy fool. Don't go staring at the weather like that. You'll get yourself killed for a-certain."

Only it wasn't the weather I had fixed in my eyesight. No, indeed. I strained against the wind and the dark to the top of that ridge. Couldn't keep from staring, right up there at the crest where I knew for sure I had seen the figure of a man standing there, still as a statue, looking down on us. The lightning came again, this time burning a hole into the very place I had seen the looker. And then, there was no one. In the time it took for me to assess the possibilities of who I had seen, the sky cleared and the day returned to our place.

Gary Wayne closed to my side. "You saw someone again, now, didn't you, Chess?"

I shrugged my shoulders.

He looked me in the eyes. "Was him, right? The one in the woods?"

I stood there, tongue-tied for an answer.

He pushed me toward the barn, where we had done a poor job with the mule and its tack. "Look here, Chess, whatever it is, we got to face it one of these days."

"We, Gary Wayne?"

"Yeah, pal, we. I ain't had so much fun since I went back for my motor scooter."

The smell of fresh earth raised our spirits. Gary Wayne and I watched Jule groom the mule. Now and then, she looked over at us as if to say, *This is how it's done, boys.*

We did, indeed, learn from her: how she took time with her chores, never throwing things about as we boys were wont to do; how she hung the tack, each piece prepared for use next time we hitched the mule to take out the wagon. I do believe she took satisfaction showing us how to handle the ropes.

After supper, we took our places on the porch that ran along the front of the cabin, looking out at "them blue mountains," as Mr. Duffy described them. He had his chair off to the side so he could prop his legs up on the rail. He drew a kitchen match across the top of the banister and lit a corncob pipe, dropping the spent match next to the porch on top of a pile of dead matches that resembled a miniature beaver dam.

As I was to learn to my disappointment later on in life, a pipe never tastes as good as it smells. It smelled good then, like age itself, rich and full of magic and tales of times I would come to know only in my reading, my imagination, and in the words of the storyteller.

CHAPTER EIGHTEEN

Time ticks, tick tock.
See the sun or hear the clock.
Now is gone forever fast,
Living ever in the past.

THE WHITE TOBACCO SMOKE curling out of Mr. Duffy's corncob pipe reminded me of the mist shrouding the mountains, layered like blue and gray mirages in front of us. Even now, if I close my eyes and allow myself, I can smell the sweet smoke floating across the porch and hear the old man tell his story:

"In 1860, when I was eleven years old, my daddy took me by the hand, and we boarded the clipper ship bound for the port of New Orleans. County Cork, we were from, County Cork, Ireland."

I computed it in my mind. One hundred and seven years old. Mr. Duffy was one hundred and seven years old. A mere ninety years older than me.

He said, "Wanted to be a sailor. Life aboard that ship was an adventure every boy should have."

The thought scared me. "Wasn't it scary?" I interrupted.

He didn't seem to mind, like Momma Opalona would have. She didn't cotton to interruptions. No, Mr. Duffy didn't mind. His eyes glittered so, I could almost see the waves carved by the bow of the sailing ship.

He looked down at me, seated on the steps below the porch. Gary Wayne leaned his back against the cabin wall under the window ledge, his knees pulled to his chest. Next to him, directly beside the old plank-bottom chair occupied by Mr. Duffy, Jule sat cross-legged, looking up at her grandfather with the same captivation she must have had the first time she heard the story. Doubtless, she had heard it many times since.

Mr. Duffy responded to my question. "It's not an adventure,

Chester, if you ain't scared."

I thought of Devil's Head and wondered if my own grandchildren would marvel at my deeds, or secretly ridicule it as the ranting of a touched old man. I sat in amazement at Mr. Duffy's exploits. By now, his voice had changed. Instead of the soft mountain drawl, an Irish brogue intoned the words, relating the past as if it were the present.

"Port o' New Orleans," he said, eliding the two words together, making it come out *Nawlins* like the Cajuns who lived there said the word. "Port o' New Orleans was a piece of magic and enchantment them days."

I had never heard the old man use the kind of words you would find in books. But when he told his stories, it was as if he read from a book. Every line seemed natural and spontaneous, but I knew for sure the next time I heard the story, it would come out the same. Same words, same sentences, same pauses, same magic and enchantment.

"Dada tried hard labor like in the Old Country. I worked beside him. But the Irish in him gained the upper hand, and he took to drinking and gambling, which was as natural to him as water." He paused so the revelation would have time to sink in.

"You would imagine," he continued, "me old daddy lost everything. Weren't so. He done well building his log cabins, and gambling on them riverboats, or in the Irish pubs or fancy casinos of the French district near the Mississippi, or anyplace—anyplace else he could find a stud poker game."

Mr. Duffy stopped and smiled. I caught those images in his eyes again. He saw memories his words couldn't properly picture. How I wanted to be an angel and fly into those eyes to see the sights that still made an old man smile.

He told his story for over an hour. All of a sudden, his face changed. I saw his eyes dim, and I knew he was coming to the part that was hard for him to tell.

"Then the war came, and we made our decision to fight for the state that took us in. Wasn't a matter of slavery for us, or who was right or wrong. We simply saw the folk we come to love make their decision to fight. It all seemed kinda natural from then on. I say *we* because there was nowhere Daddy could leave me."

Mr. Duffy laughed. "Daddy said, 'Owen. Owen,' he said, 'I'm joining up. You can stay here or come along as ya please. But, I must be honest with you, boyo, I've nowhere to place you.'"

Mr. Duffy threw back his head and laughed again. He pulled out his leather tobacco pouch and seemed to laugh into it as he dipped his pipe into the pouch, tamped the bowl with the head of his pocketknife, and pulled another match across the banister and held it to the dry leaves. His belly still bounced from laughter when the tobacco ignited, crinkling embers and smoke into the darkening sky. He looked down at all of us as if to ensure our attention. Then he continued, his Southern drawl mysteriously returning as he spoke:

"My daddy had a knack for telling things the way they were. So, I tagged along when he enlisted. Seventh Louisiana Infantry, Company G. Enlisted myself on the condition I could stay with my own daddy."

Mr. Duffy looked off into the night and moved his head away from the mountain, toward the hill where his loved ones slept. I saw a tear, which he made no effort to hide, peek over the rim of his eyelid, then slide down the old face like a raindrop riding a grain of weathered wood.

I had to ask, "What was it like, Mr. Duffy?"

He smiled down at me. "You asked me that this morning."

"Yes, sir." I had the feeling he hadn't prepared a script to answer the question.

"It was like a story in which you are the main character. Only, it didn't seem like there was ever a beginning or an end."

He looked down at his pipe. It had gone out, but he didn't bother to light it again. He said, "I still feel it like when I was twelve. You may see an old man here, but I don't feel like an old man. I hear the thunder of the cannon, muskets rattling like someone playing a tiresome, crackling tune on the tabletop. I smell the smoke drifting across what was once a field of corn. I see the faces of the other boys. A time or two, I looked for my daddy, but we got separated early. I must have looked like all the others—pale white, scared, glassy looks in our eyes. My tongue dried up. I thought I could somehow hide in my own clothes, making me invisible, so the minié balls would blow right on by me."

Mr. Duffy was not talking from a memory he had practiced. Jule's cheeks shined with the tears she had rubbed from her eyes. Gary Wayne's big eyes got bigger. Only thing that moved was the hair on my friend's head catching the warm winds pushed ahead of storm clouds moving in our direction, blowing sprinkles of rain across the porch.

ed if Mr. Duffy would go on; my own daddy refused to
Korean War. "Maybe later," Daddy often told me.
ve been later enough for Mr. Duffy. He broke the
hey started dropping beside me. The boys just dropped.
be I heard the balls slamming against them, but mostly they
dropped without any noise. If there was noise, it all seemed to stop
for me. It was like I was walking in a dream, blocking out everything but the sound of my heart. I can't remember if I even shoul-
dered my musket to put up a fight. That was the first time."

He took in a deep breath and sighed without looking down.
"After that, the next battle, I got my bearings and commenced to
work real hard at staying alive. But, it was too late for my daddy.
If his body was ever found, I did not know it."

This time, he laughed. "When I couldn't find him in the tents
taking money from the younger soldiers, I knew for sure he was
off to visit his ancestors."

For a long time he spoke no more.

I was too embarrassed to see if he was crying. Tears filled my
eyes. By then the rain came rat-a-tatting across the roof of the
porch. I felt its dampness touch me to the bone, and I pulled down
the sleeves of my cotton flannel shirt. A heaviness filled my arms
and legs.

I wondered if growing up had to be so painful. Why do people
have to kill one another? Even then, I seemed to be in touch with
the insanity of war. Mr. Duffy did not make it sound glorious. He
did touch me with its sadness.

Finally, he said, "Jule, go on in the cabin and fetch me my
papers." He said it like it was a part of the story, and Jule responded
as I was sure she had on many occasions.

In a moment, she returned and handed the old man a leather
ammunition pouch, worn to the point of coming apart like a large
jigsaw puzzle. Mr. Duffy handled it like a sacrament.

"Brung this home with me from the war," he said as he carefully pulled open the flap cover and reached inside.

They were his separation papers and a letter, from Captain
Richardy of G Company, commending Private Duffy for his service
to the cause. He read them to us. Propped his old spectacles on
his face, then read them to us. But I knew he didn't see the words
on the paper. They were in his heart, put there a long time ago on
a battlefield where boys dropped and Mr. Duffy discovered the sadness of growing up—and the sacredness of life.

CHAPTER NINETEEN

Resin up the bow,
Tune up the fiddle,
Pluck that banjo,
Hey diddle diddle.

COME ONE SUNDAY MORNING, I discovered that life in the Appalachian Mountains wasn't all work and no play. Mr. Duffy entered our quarters, all washed up and sporting a clean set of overalls and a fresh flannel shirt. "We're a-heading to church, boys," he said. "Best shed yourself of them smelly clothes and look to be gentlemen. Fact is, wouldn't hurt you none to use the trough and shed yourselves of a few weeks of dirt."

My first thought? Fear.

Church. Hey, folks go to church. Someone might recognize me. It came to me then that the fear of being recognized was something I might have to deal with for the rest of my natural life. Part of that turned out true. But not the part either Gary Wayne or I expected.

Our mouths stuck on open. Gary Wayne got out an "uhhhhh," but it didn't amount to much. We both stood there, on the edge of disbelief, watching Jule, who had turned into a for-real girl.

"Gaaa," he got out, still not able to communicate in words. "Gaaa," he repeated. He looked over at me. "You see what I see?"

I saw her, all right, coming toward us from the cabin. A real girl in a soft green dress, black patent-leather shoes, and her hair all done up in such a way as neither one of us could have figured out how she did it. Her brown eyes seemed somehow bigger, and I swear there was a touch of red on her lips I had never ever seen before. And the way she walked. And the way she smelled. And she wasn't even wearing Wild Root Hair Lotion.

I glanced over at Gary Wayne just in time to warn him: "You

are about to drool spit. I swear, Gary Wayne, she's just a girl."

But the look in his eyes told me that Jule was not just a girl to my friend.

Mr. Duffy's arrival saved us from further embarrassment, though I did notice that Jule seemed quite capable of acting as if she had no idea at all that we were staring at her. No, not a bit concerned, she seemed.

He asked us to retrieve a long wooden box from under his cot and tote the mysterious load to the wagon. He called it his music box. From the weight of it and the way he told us to take care not to drop or bump it against anything, I assumed it must have contained more than sheet music. We secured it with ropes to the front of the wagon, just under the bench.

We hitched Lamech to the wagon. This time Jule refrained from any manual task, sitting pretty as you please on the wagon seat, watching the two of us struggle with the buckles, while the mule acted indignant over our fumbling ways.

"In the back, boys," Mr. Duffy directed us.

We hoisted ourselves over the tailgate, watching him mount the wagon with the enthusiasm of a much younger man.

He whistled, said "giddyap," and slapped the reins to move Lamech into a walk. The mule's ears swept back.

Jule whispered back to us, "Watch those ears. Sure sign that old animal does not appreciate the command."

Mr. Duffy slapped the reins again and put Lamech into a trot, followed by a barely audible "We'll see who's in charge here."

We arrived at church before anyone else.

The church building stood proper, residing as it did in a deep cove, removed from the few homes that dotted the sides of the valley. Early crocuses and daffodils broke through the red clay that covered the cove. A creek ran the length of the valley, trickles of water sounding here and there as a fallen tree and river rock impeded the flow. The church spire would have looked higher, had it not been for the towering trees—old growth trees—that surrounded the wood frame structure.

"Ain't no particular church," Mr. Duffy said. He looked at us. "You boys don't mind, now, do you?" He didn't wait for us to answer. "Me, I was natural-born Catholic. Two kinds of Irish, you know. Them that's Catholic and them that ain't. I figure my saintly mother would turn in her grave, she saw me praying with all these

Protestants. Not to mention our preacher." His eyes got a twinkle to them. "Like most the folks out here, I decided I could find God wherever I happened to be. Only got one genuinely ordained preacher these parts, and the fella's a colored man. Rides his horse down here most near every month, depending on the weather." He looked at us again. "You ain't got no problems with that? And I don't mean the horse part!"

It wasn't long before they started arriving, one at a time, coming from different directions. Most on foot. Some in wagons and buggies. No automobiles. Not much of a road, even for horse-drawn transportation, to be honest.

Funny thing. Except for Jule, one boy about my age—maybe a shade younger—and now Gary Wayne and me, there were no children. All the folks had passed fifty, most older, and they seemed resigned to the loneliness of their lives in that isolated place. I lost any fear that I might be discovered.

Preacher Madden looked near as old as Mr. Duffy. His gray hair, thinning, seemed to dance in the breeze of his hand fan as he moved his head back and forth in time to the music. We sang traditional hymns and ended with "What a Friend we Have in Jesus," which preceded the sermon.

Reverend Madden rose from his chair, his body lean and bent over with age. Jule informed us that the preacher had traveled on his horse the greatest distance of all of us who gathered there.

When he spoke, he got my attention from the very first sentence: "It be the prodigal son who gots the most to lose, he ain't come back home." I swear, he looked straight into my eyes when he said, "Y'all see, now, it be the one the Lawd loves who gots the most responsibility to stop his running ways and come home to claim his reward. Course, all the reward in the whole wide world do come with responsibility. You can't has you cake and eats it, too." He laughed. "So you see now, today we all gonna set down here and asks ourselves, 'Selves, ain't you got something you needs to do? Ain't there somewheres that far-off responsibility you gots to attend to afore you reaps your just desserts?'" And then, as if the entire sermon had been prepared and directed at me, he said, "I asks y'all, now do there be a sister or brother or other childrens who be in need of your very help?"

The preacher continued. An hour or more, so as the folks would get their penny's worth. For I swear, I had never seen so many copper coins thrown into a collection basket in my life. I did not believe, though, that Preacher Madden preached for the money.

We finished with "Rock of Ages" and "Amazing Grace" and the sound of our stomachs grumbling for the smell of the food cooking under the trees outside the church.

By dusk, our stomachs settled, we all found places on the grass for the evening's entertainment. Preacher Madden sat bent forward in his chair, leaning on his Stella twelve string, looking across the valley, seemingly undistracted by the others tuning their instruments.

Donna and Frederick Minor brought their four-string banjo and mandolin. Mr. Minor had a long, curly black beard, and Donna's blue eyes almost matched the color of her simple dress, which she had starched and pressed for the occasion. I had learned that they were Mr. Duffy's closest neighbors, two miles down the trail leading into Balsam Grove. Their son, P. J., stood at attention next to a washtub and long cane, anchored together by bailing twine, that produced a bass sound, amazingly effective at keeping rhythm for the other players. He was tall with coal-black hair. His eyes were blue, and he couldn't take them off Jule. Gary Wayne took notice, because he never took his eyes off P. J.

It was then I knew for sure that Gary Wayne had developed feelings for Mr. Duffy's granddaughter. It was also then that we discovered that Mr. Duffy had what amounted to a music store of instruments in his music box.

Jule tuned a flat-top Martin, called a Baby Martin because it was considerably smaller than the other guitars from the Martin Guitar Company. Then she set up a hammer dulcimer Mr. Duffy said was old as music and came to be named for the Latin word for *sweet*. When Jule finished tuning that one, she turned to a smaller version, a lap instrument called the Appalachian dulcimer.

Mr. Duffy placed a five-string banjo next to his chair and ran his bow across a fiddle. It became evident Mr. Duffy had more talents than the expert construction of log cabins. Throughout the course of the evening, we discovered what else he had stored in the music box. Besides the two instruments at his side, he played guitar, mandolin, and a tin whistle he fiddled with when he wasn't actually fiddling the fiddle.

He looked at Gary Wayne and me. "You boys care to join in?"

I was never so grateful for my mother in my life. She'd played an old Harmony guitar down home and had hoisted it on me when I was young enough to appreciate music in a boy's life. "I can play a little rhythm on the guitar," I said.

Mr. Duffy smiled, then looked at Jule and said, "Jule, go on to the wagon there and bring this young man the Duffy from out of the music box."

The Duffy was a handmade guitar, one of several he crafted along with dulcimers and fiddles during the winter when life in the mountains slowed. He sold them to musicians from all over. I was embarrassed to even hold the instrument.

The guitar, a six stringer, boasted a spruce top from a local tree, a rosewood body, and ebony fingerboard—special woods Mr. Duffy had traded for with a cabinetmaker down in Balsam Grove. Except for a Gibson my elementary school music teacher let me touch once down in Brevard, I had never in my life put my hands on so fine an instrument.

Mr. Duffy sensed my apprehension. He said, "Go on, boy, tune her up and let's get to playing."

Get to playing, we did. We warmed up our vocal chords with "Leaving Blue" and "Good Mornin' Blues."

Preacher Madden took the lead in "Haul, Make Her Go High," a Leadbelly adaptation of a field holler about a man who escaped from slavery and prison.

Even Gary Wayne started rapping his hands on the porch, keeping time with instrumentals like "Foggy Mountain Breakdown," "Old Joe Clark," "Cripple Creek," and "Devil's Dream."

I got brave enough to take the lead on "Freight Train," one of only two simple leads I had learned from Momma. By the time the sun was down, the sound of bluegrass, folk, blues, and country music echoed across the valley like a pleasant evening shower.

Looking back, I've often wondered how much we lost when the radio and television took away the kind of entertainment we used to make for ourselves. It was the first of many Sunday night jams. I was grateful it was not the last.

Though, in the back of my mind, the words of Preacher Madden whispered another tune, one of responsibility, a kind of lingering pain in the neck that would haunt me almost as much as the fear of a man silhouetted on the top of the ridge above our place. His words would never be lost on me: "Y'all see, now, it be the one the Lawd loves who gots the most responsibility to stop his running ways and come home to claim his reward."

When he was ready to leave, he climbed on his horse and looked down at me. Picked me out of the crowd, he did. "Come here, now, boy, I gots something to tell you." He looked the others off, and I walked by his side as he urged his mount down the trail away from the church. "You listening, now, ain't you, boy?"

"Yes, sir."

"You know it do get dark out hereabouts on my way back home. I trusts the Lawd, understand, but that ain't save me from the fear and trepidations that the devil casts my way. You take that mountain yonder Brevard way. You know which one I mean?"

"Yes, sir."

"Well, there be times, I swear, I see them creatures glow in the night. Up there in the woods, I see them glow a kind of yellow-green. You do know what I mean, now don't you?"

"Yes, sir."

"You sure one polite boy."

"Yes, sir."

"Well, now, I ain't got no business telling you what you got to do. No sir, no business at all. But the Lawd . . . well, the Lawd do make demands of thems he loves. Uh-huh?"

"Yes, sir."

"That's right. So, I hears from folks that you be sent off to the reformatory, accounta they said you done harm to some of your friends up on that mountain. They say you crazy and claims it weren't you. No sir, not you a'tall. Course, someone who has seen them creatures glowing up on that mountain, he be inclined to believe you, uh-huh."

"You're not going to tell—"

"No sir. I come to preach, that's all. Course, you did hear my word today?"

"Yes, sir."

"One these days, you know what you gots to do."

"Yes, sir."

I watched him down the trail until he faded into the shadows.

That's when I realized that I had walked a good half mile or so away from the church and the others. The darkness fell, but not before I felt a presence in the woods. It took every inch of courage I could muster not to run wildly back up the trail. He followed me, step for step, just out of my sight, but not out of my awareness. Just then it came to me that the fear of what you cannot see is the worst fear of all.

CHAPTER TWENTY

When I am ten and seventy,
I know that I will find
A secret place of fantasy
Kept hidden in my mind.
And in my heart I'll keep our secret
Safe behind my gate,
Sealed with your tender kisses once
When I was ten and eight.

I SHOULDN'T HAVE been surprised when Gary Wayne fell in love with Jule. She was, even at sixteen, a remarkable girl. Gary Wayne told me so. That's when I figured out what he would have denied: He had fallen for her like lightning from a thunderhead.

"Know what?" he said to me. "Jule is gonna be a doctor."

That did come as a revelation to me, along with the fact that she went to school every morning before Gary Wayne and I even got up for our chores.

He showed me the "schoolhouse" behind the cabin. I had always assumed it was a summer kitchen no longer used. I was partially right. It had been a summer kitchen, used by the deceased Mrs. Duffy. Now it was a school. Gary Wayne showed me inside.

I was surprised. It *was* a school. Inside the twelve-by-twelve cabin sat a desk, bookshelves filled with books of all kinds, a small black coal heater, a globe of the world, and maps covering the walls from top to bottom.

He explained it to me the way Jule had told him: "She said she had something to show me," Gary Wayne said. "I said okay, thinking maybe she had a treasure box hidden somewhere like girls do to keep their play-pretties in. I was wrong. She took me into this cabin. She said, 'This is my school. Except weekends, I get up every morning before chores and come in here to do my work.'"

"What work?" I interrupted, still not getting it.

He answered, "School work. Jule told me, 'I'm gonna be a doctor by and by. You just wait and see.'"

I interrupted Gary Wayne again. "She said she's going to be a doctor?"

He nodded his head. "That's right, Chess, a doctor. Said it all started before her momma died. She was sick. Her momma was sick, see. Jule never left her side. She cared for her and tended to her illness. Jule said Doc Cannon used to come visit her momma all the time she was sick. One day, he says to her, 'Jule, I do believe that one of these days, you are going to be the first woman doctor in these parts.'"

Gary Wayne smiled like he was proud of Jule himself.

A genuine sign of true love, I thought. I had heard of Dr. Gaine Cannon. If there ever was a saint in these hills, he fit the bill. All the mountain folk revered the man. For him to say something like that to Jule must have sounded like a prophecy. Leastwise, she took it to be.

According to Gary Wayne, Jule had her mind made up. "Look around you, Chess," he said. "See them science and medical books and such. She says Mr. Duffy made this room up special for her. He went down to the school in Brevard and borrowed textbooks so she could keep up with her schooling right here. Doc Cannon let her have these other books so she could prepare for becoming a doctor."

I said, "How you suppose she can do that?" thinking how hard it was for me in school, and how I secretly dreaded going back because of all the lessons I missed at the reformatory. School there had been something like a bad joke. If you tried to learn, the other boys made fun of you. So you gave up trying.

Gary Wayne did not take kindly to my skepticism. "She just does, Chess. Twice a year, Mr. Duffy takes her down to Brevard for testing. Jule says she's ahead of the other kids there, on account of her determination."

Gary Wayne set his jaw when he said the word *determination*. I was beginning to believe him.

I inspected some of the books, tried to read aloud one of the titles. "Path...o...phy..., pathophy...si, pathophysio...logy, pathophysiology." I couldn't pronounce it, much less understand what it meant.

Gary Wayne flashed his I-told-you-so smile.

From that day on, I knew I would have to watch myself around

Jule. Gary Wayne had taken to her. Then, there was the summer afternoon, while I was lying on my stomach down by the creek, watching water spiders and dragonflies dance across the stream, that I found out the feeling was mutual.

I heard them coming up from the trail that led along the stream. I was on the bank, hidden by ground fern and mountain laurel. It was my meditation time, although I didn't call it that back then. The dogwoods and azaleas had blossomed, their delicate pink and white flowers locking their wild smell in my memory.

I heard Gary Wayne and Jule talking, and by the time I discovered the conversation was personal, I had to choose between embarrassing them or appearing that I was listening in on purpose—which, I suppose, I was.

Gary Wayne had his thumbs locked in the straps of his overalls. He tossed his head to throw the hair out of his eyes. I could tell someone had played with it. Gary Wayne always kept his hair combed neatly, with a careful part down the side. That part no longer existed.

Jule wore a dress. Oh, yes, her simple blue shift and bare feet stood out against the deep forest green. When the wind caught her dress, it left no doubt she didn't look anything like a slight kid the first time I saw her cradling a J. C. Higgins rifle. No doubt, that was the very reason she wore it. Freckles sprinkled across her nose and cheeks playfully. She no longer cut her hair short. It now hung past her shoulders, thick, deep brown, some strands light as corn silk in the spring sunshine. My friend did not stand a chance.

Jule said, "Gary Wayne, I like it when you hold my hand."

He got the hint and took her hand in his. I could almost imagine his face turning red, like it did when he had dropped his trousers before he knew Jule was a girl.

Gary Wayne didn't say anything, so Jule said, "Do you suppose we will be friends forever?"

He said, "Sure!"

A man of many words, I decided.

"You're not saying so 'cause you think I want you to, are you, Gary Wayne?" She said his name with a kind of sweetness I had never heard from her before.

Poor old Gary Wayne, I thought, *you can kiss your freedom goodbye. That girl's set her sights on you and is just about to squeeze the trigger.*

By then I could see them together through the ferns. They had sat down on the footbridge that crossed the creek about twenty yards from where I lay. Their legs hung over the side, and they swung them back and forth as their arms leaned over the middle rail.

Gary Wayne looked like he wanted to spit in the water, but he thought better of it when Jule smiled at him and cradled her head against his shoulder. She reached up and twisted a lock of his hair playfully in her fingers. His ears turned beet red. I saw him swallow hard. He did manage to reach over and pat her hands that were now entwined around his arm.

That's right, Gary Wayne, I thought, *you go on and show her you're in charge.*

Jule said, "I never felt like this with another boy."

Gary Wayne swallowed again. "You didn't?" he said. I knew what he wanted to say. He wanted to say, *You never felt like what with another boy?*

I wanted to whisper in his ear, *Gary Wayne, the only other boy she's even been around is old P. J. Minor, and all he ever did was grin at her whilst he was plunking that washtub bass.* But it was too late for Gary Wayne.

Jule could have said, *Jump off a cliff for me, Gary Wayne,* and he would have asked her, *Which one, honey?* She held him steady with her eyes while she lined him up for what I suspected was his first-ever kiss. I felt a tingling down my back and wondered what poor Gary Wayne must have been feeling all the time Jule edged her mouth closer to his.

Don't do it, Gary Wayne.

Too late.

She smacked him right on the lips, soft at first, then harder. He was barefoot, so I saw his toes curl up like he'd received a jolt of electricity.

It was over. I was relieved, sort of. But I knew for sure that while Gary Wayne and I would be friends for life, I would have to get in line.

The next kiss came compliments of Gary Wayne.

I made the mistake of chuckling out loud, and the race was on. He was bigger than me, but I was faster and quicker. He almost caught me in the stream but fell on his face.

I did myself no favors taunting him: "I sure do like it when you hold my hand, Gary Wayne."

"I'm gonna kill you, Chess."

"Your kisses sure are sweet."

"I'm gonna kill you, Chess, for sure. Can't run forever."

"Can too."

"Keep running, you little coward. One of these days—"

"One of these days, I'm gonna get you to teach me how to kiss all the girls."

All the time, Jule's yelling at Gary Wayne to stop chasing me, and hollering, "Come back here right now, you hear?"

For the rest of that summer, Jule and Gary Wayne learned about puppy love. I learned how to build log cabins, keep my mouth shut about my friends, and talk to waterbugs and dragonflies. I had almost forgotten the pains of missing my family and the terror of losing a friend to circumstances no one would believe.

I was happy for my two new friends, but a restlessness tugged at my conscience. Preacher Madden's words had been aimed directly at me. I just knew they were. Hannah Jane was still a captive.

Though I was almost at peace, I knew my retreat would have to come to an end. I wasn't prepared for the way it did.

CHAPTER TWENTY-ONE

There is another adventure still,
Awaiting 'cross the distant hill.
Set sail beyond the clouds somewhere.
Close your eyes,
Quiet your fears,
Your dreams will take you there.

IT WAS GETTING ON TO AUTUMN. Soon the hunter's moon would bring out the deer and predators. And the aliens. I had not seen another shadow in the woods nor a figure on the ridge, but he came to me in my dreams. He waited out there in the woods, staying around time to time, not to harass nor harm me. No, I had figured it out. I would be safe, as long as I remained where I was, the prodigal son wasting away in exile.

The time came when I asked Gary Wayne if he would mind were I to leave on my own and see what I could do for my friend on Devil's Mountain.

But Gary Wayne had not forgotten his promise. This time, he said he would go with me. "I suppose I got to admit that you ain't the kind to make up such a story if it ain't true."

"You're just trying to be nice," I said, "what you said before, about taking me along because I begged and such. Well, I wouldn't blame you for staying here and. . . ."

He understood that I understood about Jule and him. "Yeah, well, a buddy don't run out on a buddy when the going gets tough."

"I don't know, Gary Wayne. This is my own doing, and I just sort of figured I ought to be the one to work it out."

"Now, you don't want my help? You telling me you don't want me to help you out with them . . . ah . . . them . . . well, you know?"

"That is exactly what bothers me. You can't even say the word. You can't say the word. You think I been seeing too many Martian picture shows."

"Not lately." He laughed.

I could feel my face turn red. "You still don't believe me. You don't believe a word of it, not even Momma Opalona's story." I felt foolish. Defending myself again. I didn't want to feel that.

Made me think of Yancey Larson, my daddy's brother's friend, who once worked on the atom bomb over in New Mexico. "A genius," Daddy had said of him. "A nut, too."

Of course, Daddy had every right to say so. The lean, gaunt fellow would come along with my uncle sometimes when he visited us. The man had rocks bulging from his pants, shirt, and coat pockets. When he would sit down, he would take a few out of his pocket and place them at the table where he drank his coffee—or anyplace he happened to sit, for that matter. Right in front of him, the rocks.

Once, when the other grownups had gone out to see one of Daddy's "new" used cars, Aldous asked the man, "Hey, Mr. Yancey, how come you got all those rocks in your pockets and such?"

I stood in the background waiting for him to put Aldous in his place. He did not. Instead, he had the both of us join him at the kitchen table, where he explained in a perfectly logical way how it was that aliens had invaded our planet Earth and how they could only be kept at a distance with a certain kind of river rock that you had to harvest in the dark of night so the alien fellows didn't see you doing it.

When Aldous said, "That's crazy, Mr. Yancey," I almost fell out of the chair for fear of what the man might do to us.

He did nothing. Instead, he picked up a couple of those river rocks and gave one to each of us. "Now boys," he said, "you don't want to take a chance the aliens from outer space will take you hostage in their spaceships, do you?"

The more I thought about it, the more sense it made. That night, lying awake in our bed, Aldous summed it up for me. "Hey, Chess, you know how Daddy won't go nowhere without that rabbit foot he carries on his key chain?"

"Yeah." I knew I had just been convinced to hold on to that river rock.

Aldous made it sound simple. "Well, it ain't nothing but a little old rock, you know."

I don't know how long we carried those river rocks around with us in the pockets of our trousers. I do remember regretting it one evening when Daddy told us at the supper table, "Yancey Larson got himself in a whole world of hurt with the law."

We couldn't wait for the punch line.

My mother said, "We don't want to discuss that here, now, do we."

It was not a question. Still, Daddy risked her wrath and told us, "Man went downtown to the sheriff's office. Walked right on in, dropped his trousers and drawers, and mooned the desk sergeant."

Aldous said, "What's *moon* mean?"

Momma said, "Never mind."

Daddy said, "He told the deputy that if they let him out of jail, he'd do it again and again till they put him right back. Something to do with jail being the one place that would be safe enough when the Martian invasion takes place."

Daddy laughed. Momma frowned. Aldous and I excused ourselves from the table so we could run outside and get rid of our river rocks. I do recall Aldous asked me, also, "What's moon mean?"

Someone told me that they took away his rocks, but the man said that would be okay because he had a backup plan. That time on, it was said that Yancey Larson never went anywhere without sugar in his pockets.

The thought that someone—especially my best friend—would think I was as crazy as Yancey was almost too much. The embarrassment of it almost made me decide against leaving.

Though I loved the mountains, those were not the best of times for me. I missed my momma and daddy and Aldous. On the other hand, I was safe, somewhat at peace, and not at all sure of what to do about it. Mr. Duffy helped me make up my mind.

He sat on the log, balancing it while I sawed. Mr. Duffy said that old men make perfect log sitters, on account of they got nothing but time. He said I wouldn't appreciate that fully till I was older. He then reflected on my uneasiness. "I can see you gazing off to them mountains a mite, boy. You got business pressing." He was not asking. He pointed out what I didn't want to admit.

I stopped my work. "Yes, sir, I reckon I do. Just not sure I'm up to it."

He said, "No one's gonna make you do anything you don't want to. Not up here, anyway, Chester. Except maybe yourself."

He was right. It was my choice. Just not an easy one. I figured I could go right on living up there on that mountain, doing what I enjoyed for the rest of my life. But. . . .

I said to him, "Mr. Duffy, you ever done something you didn't want to do, but you did it 'cause you felt obligated?" I knew what he would say, soon as I said it.

"You know the answer to that one, Chester. You're dead right. Ain't easy. Recollect the first time I stepped out onto that field of mortal combat, I says to myself, 'Owen, boy, you ain't gonna come through this one alive.' Then I says, 'Why you doing this?'" He looked at me holding the cross saw ready for another pull. Then he laughed and said, "'I don't know why I'm doing this,' I says back to myself. 'But I suppose I would feel worse if I didn't than if I did.'"

While I chewed on that, Mr. Duffy got up off the log and came over to me. He took the saw out of my hand and turned me to the valley, the direction of Brevard, the direction of Devil's Mountain. He lifted his arm and pointed where I looked. "See out there, boy. That be your field of battle. Listen to what I have to say, now. The important part is not how you do it, or what happens as a result. The important part is that you believe in what you're a-fixing to do, then you step out into the smoke and cannon fire and roll of muskets, and give it a try. If that's what you believe is right, then you step out and try. Sure enough, it may get too hot and you'll have to run back. But that ain't cause for shame. Shame comes with not trying." He laughed. "After all, we did lose the whole bloody war, didn't we? Lost it bad, son. But we stepped out onto that field. Some ran. Some died. We all, both sides, lost. Some decided it weren't worth the fight and went on and did something else. That took courage, too—I mean those boys who decided not to fight because they believed the killing was wrong. But they paid the price, too. Some killed by firing squad. Others, worse—being called cowards for doing what they believed was right."

He pulled me around by the shoulders so I faced him straight on. "Those who chose not to fight had they reasons. So you see, it takes courage either way. The important part is, you got to do what you believe is right. Either way, you will know you been in a fight."

We were set to leave in the morning. I had swallowed my pride and asked Gary Wayne, "Would you come with me, even though I know you don't completely believe what I say I saw?"

He said, "Would you do that for me?"

We both knew the answer.

Saying goodbye was not a skill Gary Wayne had developed. Jule cried. He said he would be back before long. Jule cried some more. Gary Wayne fumbled for words that would not have consoled Jule, had he found them. They agreed to try it again in the morning.

Mr. Duffy seemed prepared. He thanked us with a cache of dollar bills he had set aside as "bonus money," for our trip. He donated a horsehair knapsack for food and extra clothes. But our journey wouldn't be far. We had, in fact, already come a long way that summer.

I dreamed about it my last evening there. Dreamed, as I sat on the porch of Mr. Duffy's cabin, looking across the valley at the mountains now in their glory. Ridges of reds, yellows, greens, oranges, browns, and purples changed their hues with the descent of the sun on its journey to the sea. I smelled the crisp break of fall, felt an energy animate my soul. That's when I knew there was a reason for the journey I had undertaken with my friend, my adopted grandfather, and his brown-eyed great-granddaughter who was like a sister to me now.

"You got to stop, sometimes," Mr. Duffy said to us. "This old body don't work on food alone. It's the blessing of age. The body stops and the soul takes over."

I can smell his pipe smoke now, see it drifting over his head like a halo above the saints. It was the last story time. He knew we would never see him again, though I assured him we would return soon as our deed was done. But he knew better. So the last story time was his final message to us—his blessing.

It was a simple message. "Stop along the way," he said. "Take time out for yourselves. Your loved ones will understand. A body's got to find itself in this world, plant its feet firmly on the ground, so it can enter peacefully into the next world. That's why I lived so long. That's why I got no regrets." He said it like it was past. I had the feeling he not only told us how to live our lives, he was saying good-bye.

Jule held his hand. He said he was tired, so she and Gary Wayne helped him into the cabin. That left me on the porch, looking at the mountains in the twilight, wondering what the morning would bring.

In a few minutes I heard Mr. Duffy snoring. He was at rest.

The sound of sobbing from inside the cabin broke into my thoughts. Jule was crying.

Gary Wayne tried to reassure her. "I promise I'll be back soon as Chess and I take care of our business." He hadn't told her about

Devil's Mountain. I had asked him to keep it a secret.

Jule blew her nose and said, "You know I wouldn't let you go without me, weren't it for Grandpa."

This parting was not easy for her. I thought of my parents, my brother, and even Hannah Jane, who was no longer someone for whom I felt a childhood crush. She was a friend in trouble. I wanted to do what I must do to try to help her. But for now, my mind drifted to Jule's and Gary Wayne's pain. Moisture filled my eyes, and I walked down the trail so I could be alone.

In the morning, Gary Wayne and I found them up the hill. Mr. Duffy had climbed there by himself sometime in the night. Jule sat next to him. She told us she discovered him there, lying across the grave of his wife, his worn leather ammunition pouch clutched in one hand, a tiny gold ring in the other.

I always believed he chose his time to die. Jule would be loved, someone there for her during the grief and after, when she longed for someone's nearness.

We buried him next to his loved ones, boarded up the cabin, and left the mountain. Gary Wayne and Jule said they would come back. But that promise would not ease the grief.

We took our grief with us, and the stories. We took the stories where *always* lives within the past, so long as there are those to tell of it.

PART III
Return to Devil's Mountain

CHAPTER TWENTY-TWO

The mind's a book of images
Floating round and round.
The storyteller shakes her mind,
And then she writes it down.
She spills the words upon the paper,
Recollecting all
The songs and rhymes and memories
Of stories, short and tall.

MOMMA OPALONA didn't look the least surprised to see me. It had been a day's walk from the mountain to her cabin at the edge of Brevard. We had bedded down in the woods until morning, so as to avoid being seen by anyone. The sun crested the eastern ridge. Down the holler, dawn showed only her fingertips.

Golden-yellow light from the coal-oil lamp spilled out the open door of Momma Opalona's place. "Bring you friends in, Chester," she said. Her voice still crackled with authority.

She had lost weight. Surprised me. I didn't think she could ever look older than the last time I saw her. But she did. Her calico dress hung loosely from her body. She stooped lower than I thought anyone could and still stay on two feet. I wondered if instead of dying, she might one day just waste away and cease filling the space around her.

Inside the shack, my interests turned to more urgent concerns. The first thing I did was look over at the coal stove and search for the bread. Old habits are the hardest ones to kill.

Momma Opalona knew that. That's why she said, "Go on, now, help you'selves."

I didn't need to explain anything to her. As usual, she already knew about me. She said, "Preacher Madden says you plays a respectable rhythm guitar." She saw my eyes get wider. "Don't worry, Chester. The reverend know it be none his business. Truth be known, it came to me one night whilst I was a-dreaming in my bed yonder, that one my childrens was in more trouble 'n you can throw a stick at. I sees him there upon that yonder mountain, and he ain't in no hurry to come on down. Appears to me, he gots some things he ain't done. You understand, now, a body gots things he ain't done, they gonna haunt him for the rest of his natural life and then some. So, I sends my messengers to tell that old man lives on that mountain where y'all been a-staying, and I tells him, my Chester has gots responsibilities. That be a big old word for things a body gots to do. Then I tells the preacher, he gots to explain it to you in words you can understand."

She looked me in the eye, that way she had of holding someone's attention whether he liked it or not. "You gots no reason to worry. The reverend ain't tell no one. He ain't reported to no one but my very own self. That's 'cause he know, you one my special childrens."

I felt my heart warm and had to work hard to keep the tears from slipping out of my eyes. I hadn't done a lot of that lately. Crying, I mean. I made myself save it for later. Just now, I needed the kind of help only Momma Opalona could give me.

I said, "Momma Opalona, so, I guess you know what happened to Hannah Jane."

She nodded. She didn't say *I told you so*, just nodded and waited for me to get to the point.

"I aim to get her back," I said. "My friends here aim to help me. But you're the only one who knows enough about those creatures to tell us how."

She looked at Jule and Gary Wayne, then back at me. We were not an impressive lot to behold. Jule's brown eyes looked swollen and red from the sadness she suffered losing her last remaining relative. With a woodsman cap hiding her tucked-up hair, and overalls covering a simple flannel shirt, she still could have passed for a teenage boy.

I closed my eyes, and in my mind, I saw her wearing that fancy dress for the first time, trying hard to impress Gary Wayne before he admitted he had fallen for her. When I opened my eyes, Jule seemed tired. Not from the trek down the mountain. Her depression came from the pain of loss. I worried that she would not be ready for the coming adventure Gary Wayne had tried to explain on our hike to Momma Opalona's shack.

Gary Wayne seemed his usual dependable self. He never looked tired. I doubt he would have let on if he were. It occurred to me how he now looked older than his seventeen years. He would be responsible for Jule now, and me. I knew Gary Wayne would have chosen to remain on the mountain, had it not been for our friendship. I prayed he would be allowed to return there once our journey ended.

I must have matured, as well. Momma Opalona had to crane her neck to see my face. Had it not been for the tightness of my clothes, I might not have noticed that I had grown several inches over the year. I felt older, too. Ready to confront the demons that forced my life to take a strange twist. I wanted to take my place back home. But I couldn't do it without trying to free my friend.

Momma Opalona had observed us long enough. She understood what we meant to do. But for the first time since I had known the woman, I got the impression that she was at a loss for words. Maybe the look in her eyes said something to me. Maybe her age had finally caught up to her.

She smiled. "You be reading my mind, now, ain't you, Chester?"

My neck burned. "Ma'am?"

"You gots that gift, you know."

"Momma Opalona, I don't—"

"Lawze no, course you don't. No one gots the gift knows 'bout it. Now, don't go getting a-scared on me. You ain't yet to develop it. No sir, not yet, not by a long stretch. Most folks gots the gift don't never practice to develop it. But they gots it, all the same."

"But, Momma—"

"But, but, but. That all you gots to say. How 'bouts you tell me what I be about to tell you young'ns. You go on and tell me now."

My mind locked up as tight as my mouth. She smiled. "You done decide that old Momma Opalona ain't rightly remembering all that well just now. Ain't that right, Chester?"

I nodded, my face full red by now. I could feel my ears burning and tried not to look at the others. I got out a whispery "Yes, ma'am."

"Well, then, you be exactly right. I knows they's something, something my very own momma said to me 'bout them aliens. But for the life of me, I can't rightly recall what it be."

We waited. Momma Opalona had closed her eyes and lowered her head. She seemed to nestle deeper into her feather mattress.

Gary Wayne whispered, "She all right, Chess?"

I whispered back, "She does this. I mean, she sometimes just goes off somewhere in her mind—"

"To the Lawd," Momma Opalona corrected me. "I goes off to the

Lawd, so's he can tell me what I gots to do."

We waited. Outside, sounds of life had wakened to the morning. I could hear mockingbirds hiss at an intruder. A whippoorwill *hoo-hooed* to its mate. Songbirds contributed to the chorus. We waited still.

Then she lifted her head and said a name: "Mullins."

I said, "Ma'am?"

"Mullins. The hermit. You knows the one I mean, Chester."

"Yes, ma'am. Denny Mullins, the hermit. I know about him."

What I knew was legend, mostly. He went by a more descriptive name in our parts—The Man Who Eats Children. I didn't believe it. I mean, I didn't believe that he actually ate children. But some did. That was good enough for me to keep away from the part of the woods where they said he roamed. Not all that difficult. Mostly, he was said to have inhabited places where no one would want to go anyway.

Momma Opalona interrupted my recollections. "You'ns gots to find him. I reckon they no other way."

"But Momma—"

"No other way, now, Chester. That man come back from the war in Europe. He gots a bad reputation, and I figures he wants it that way. But the man knows all they be to knows round 'bout these parts. He knows 'bout the ways of the woods, and I reckon he surely knows all 'bout them vampires what inhabits the top of that evil mountain."

She paused and looked directly into Gary Wayne's eyes. "That be the very truth, sir, 'bout them alien vampires, I mean. See, my very own momma be the only one to escape. . . . I take that back. Now they be two: my momma and you friend there." She nodded toward me. "He don't lie, and neither do I. You understands?"

Gary Wayne nodded.

"You do understands?"

"Yes, ma'am, I do."

"There." She looked at me. "Now you friend believes you. Ain't that a good feeling?"

"Yes, ma'am. It is."

She eased off her bed and used her staff to help her stand. "Now, whilst you young'ns runs on off to find Mullins, I be here with the Lawd, asking him why he ain't let me remember something I knows be important. Real important. Something my very own momma told me . . . 'bout them aliens folks." She escorted us to the door. "Come on back, y'all, just as soon as you meets up with that Mullins fella. Tell him I sends my best regards. Tell him I reckon he ain't as alone as he believes he is. Do that, now, hear?"

Gary Wayne said, "Now what are we going to do, Chess? I mean, this is your part of the country. You tell us."

He had me there. I had the same question he had. How in the world were we going to find a man who probably wouldn't want to be found in the first place?

Then I took a page out of Momma Opalona's book. I sat down, said, "Got to think about this one." And I did. At first, nothing came to me. So I figured maybe I ought to close my eyes and daydream, to see where they would lead me.

At first I got nowhere with that either. Then I found my mind wandering off somewhere in the woods. Before long, it came to me. Right out of my daydream, it came to me.

"You know," I said, "I just got to thinking about the time my daddy took me hunting. My very first time, ever, hunting. I mean, he had showed me how to use the rifle and all. Took plenty time with it, telling me the rules, saying as how the rules weren't no different from the BB gun he gave me a few years earlier, and how I didn't ever point it at nothing I did not intend to shoot, and how I was to never point it at another human being; and when I reminded him how he had been in Korea and all, he said that was all the more reason not to use a rifle on another human being—"

"Chess." Jule seldom spoke her mind. This time she made an exception. "Do you think that you would mind, very much . . . I mean, why don't you get to the point."

Gary Wayne said, "Yeah, get to the point, Chess."

"Okay, I'm getting there—"

"Now." Their voices rang together as if they had known each other for years and suffered the same frustrations.

"Okay. Daddy said only a fool crashes through the woods stirring up the animals and such so as he can find him a buck to take." I puffed out my chest, impressed with my observation.

"So?" Again, together.

"Okay. Daddy said that if you want to find something you're hunting, you got to wait until it finds you."

They looked at each other and nodded as if I had actually made sense.

"So, how we going to do that?" Gary Wayne asked.

How we did it was to tramp on down to the neck of the woods where everyone said we should not go, on account of that's where the man who eats children lives.

On the way, we announced to everyone we encountered that that's what we were up to. I mean, every farm and farmhand and kid on a bicycle and farmer on his mule or tractor got the message. We made it sound important.

"A quest," Jule concluded.

We were on a quest and would not stop until we found old Denny Mullins. Yessir, we exuded courage. Three knights errant on a quest.

And our courage held out, too. Until we actually found ourselves deep in those very woods that Denny Mullins called home.

Night fell hard. So, too, our spirits.

Jule said, "I'm hungry."

Gary Wayne said, "I suppose it did not occur to us that knights need food."

She did not consider his comment humorous. "What do you mean by that remark, sir."

I noted that she had dropped the *honey* from his title. I found myself moving farther and farther from the campsite we had selected for ourselves.

"Hey, I didn't mean nothing by it. Don't go getting—"

Jule said, "Getting? What do you mean *getting*, sir? If you mean that I'm acting like a girl, well—"

"I never said that, nuh-uh, never said that, no way, not at—" He stopped when he saw the tears trickle from her closed eyes. "Ah, gee whiz, Jule, I didn't mean to hurt you. I never . . . I mean I would . . . I'm sorry, really sorry."

She broke into a sob, to which Gary Wayne responded by standing there with his mouth open.

He looked at me. I shrugged. We both stood there, our collective open mouths full of nothing but air. Finally she pulled out a handkerchief and blew her nose. Then she looked at Gary Wayne, who cocked his head as if to ask *Now what.*

"Oooh, hug me," she ordered. He hugged her. "I'm so tired and hungry, and I miss my grampa, and ooooh."

That night I dreamed of bacon cooking in a skillet. The kind of bacon that sits sweet on your tongue and seems to satisfy all the way down. And coffee, too. I dreamed of coffee brewing and. . . .

I opened my eyes when the smell got so powerful that I knew I could sleep no more for the hunger my dream whetted. A blurry vision took shape: A man knelt over a campfire, slouch hat pulled down over his eyes, scraggly black beard growing from a ruddy face. When he turned to look at me, his blue eyes told me we had been found. Oh, yes, found for sure. I said a quick prayer for the bacon that was indeed frying in the pan and for the fact it was only bacon.

"Best wake the others," he said. "Reckons they ought to be hungry. Now, suppose you tell me what kind of fools would take to these woods with nothing but their big boastful mouths to protects them?"

A long rifle leaned against a fallen tree trunk that had acted as a support for the branches we used to shelter us during the night. He looked at me looking at it. "Don't fret, boy. I ain't gonna kill you'ns. Not yet, leastwise. But I do want to know what brings the three of you out here to these parts, telling everybody how you come to fetch me."

By now, Gary Wayne and Jule had wakened. They lay there snuggled near each other, their eyes focused on the man.

"Well," he said, "I am waiting for an answer. Better be good. You do know what the folks hereabouts say about my peculiar eating habits?"

"Sir."

"Yes?"

"Well, sir . . . I . . . ah . . . we come down here on account of . . . well, 'cause Momma Opalona said we should."

That one got him. I could tell. He recovered, acting as if he had known it all along, but I could tell he did not. "That so?" he said.

"Yes, sir."

"Well, boy, you a-fixing to tell me why she send you to me?"

"Yes, sir."

"I am hearing a whole passel of 'yessirs,' and that's about all. Now, boy, suppose you go on and tell me why Momma Opalona sent you to me. You know, like an explanation . . . and don't say 'yessir.' Say why you here in the first place."

"Yes . . . I mean, we come to find out about the alien creatures on Devil's Mountain." I said the words real fast, hoping he wouldn't have time to hear exactly what I said and, again, hoping he would.

"Well, why didn't you say so?" He lifted the pan from the fire and motioned with his head for us to join him at the campfire. He laid the pan down in the middle of the three of us.

He did not have to say "eat." We figured that one out all by our-selves, pulling hot bacon from the skillet, nibbling off the ends like we hadn't eaten in . . . well, it was most near a day.

He confirmed what Momma Opalona had told me and Hannah Jane so many years ago, summarizing it, and concluding with "I recollect this story as Momma Opalona told it to me when I was a boy." So, he, too, had dared to enter the realm of the legendary storyteller, a sure sign of the man's disdain for danger.

"Mr. Mullins," I said, "Momma Opalona said there's part of the story she couldn't recall."

"Like, for instance?"

"Like, what would a fella have to do if he wanted to go on up on that mountain and free a friend from—"

"That ain't what you're considering is it, boy? I mean, you ain't—all of you, I mean—all of you ain't that stupid you would want to go on up that mountain lessen you got yourselves captured and had no choice in the matter. You'ns can't be that stupid?"

I said, "Yes, sir."

He laughed loud enough that the wild things started to stir and move about in the woods out of our sight. He assessed our seriousness and said, "Yes, I do believe you intend to go up there, for a-certain. Hmmmmmmm."

"Mr. Mullins," I said, "I already been up there."

His eyes got big, and I swear he looked impressed. "You ain't lying?"

"No, sir. I ain't lying."

He smiled at me and put a hand on my shoulder, his eyes peer-ing directly into mine. "Well, boy, that makes two of us. Now, what is it I can tell you that you don't already know?"

"I want to bring a friend back."

He kept his eyes on mine. "Now, that is a mystery, ain't it?"

He slapped his hands and stood. His eyes scanned the woods. "Y'all do know someone's been following you, don't you? You know someone dogging your trail all the time since you entered these woods."

My heart thumped. All three of us said "no" at the same time. Gary Wayne looked at me and nodded. He believed me. Now, he believed me for sure.

"I think it's one of them," I said. "The boy who trapped us. He got Hannah Jane, but I ran away. I mean, I escaped. They just about caught me, though."

Mr. Mullins let me off easy. "I'da run, too, boy. Me, I found them on my own. No one seen me. Slipped up there on the full moon, just like Momma Opalona said I shouldn't oughta do. Yessir, found them alien fellows and saw them children too. Found them, but they did not find me. You musta been a-scared in the presence of them creatures."

I looked over at my friends. I suppose it did pleasure me to see the looks on their faces when he described the aliens he had seen when he was also a mere boy. Just like I remembered.

"Round heads," he said. "Lit up kinda yellow and green when they did their ceremony under that full moon. Yessir, I'da shivered in my boots, I'da had any on. They never did see me. Never acknowledged my presence, leastwise. But times are, I get the feeling they're all around me here in these dark places." He shivered. We shivered. "Now, I do reckon one of them is traipsing here about, to be sure. Fellow who tailed the three of you all the way up here."

"You saw him?"

"Naw. I heard him. He hightailed it when it came to him that I was doing the same thing to him that he was doing to you."

Small favors, I thought. But I had to pin him down. I had to find out if Mr. Mullins knew something that could help us. "Sir, you said you heard the same tale from Momma Opalona as she told me."

"That's right."

"Then, maybe there's something she told you that she forgot to tell us."

"Boy, you keep thinking like that, you most likely amount to something one these days."

We compared stories. Nothing different. Momma Opalona had her facts straight. Same story. That is, till the very end, when Mr. Mullins asked me, "She did show you inside that old steamer trunk of hers, now didn't she?"

I thought about it. "No, sir. She said something like, one of these days she would do just that."

"Well, boy, I do recommend that you pose it to her that it's about time she opened up that old trunk of hers. You just might be surprised what she finds in there."

He sent us packing—full stomachs, and full of wonder about the alien creatures, and full of wonder about what it was Momma Opalona had hidden in her old steamer trunk. What he did not do was relieve us of the fear that John Croshaw would soon pick up our trail.

CHAPTER TWENTY-THREE

What lies inside that hidden box
Where memories are stored?
A sash or slouch hat full of holes
Or rusted cavalry sword
Or maybe matters deeper still
Than artifacts of war,
Perhaps a book of memories
Of magic, myth, or more.
For if the past is presently
A mystery to find,
Perhaps a jostle here and there
Might bring the truth to mind.

AN "UHHH-HMMMMMM" came out of her mouth. "That what Mullins say? You sure that what he say?"

We nodded.

Momma Opalona looked at me. "Chester, you positive I ain't already done that. I mean, you knows for sure I ain't already showed you the content of my treasure chest?"

"Momma Opalona, you said that one day you would show us what's inside."

She sighed. "Well then, I suppose this be the day."

It seemed to take her longer than I remembered to ease herself out of her great bed. She finally balanced her body with the story staff and shuffled slowly over to the trunk at the foot of her bed. She tapped it with her stick like she had done when we first visited her. I half expected the lid to fly open revealing dragons and spirits of wizards and storytellers past. It didn't.

"Get on over here, Chester. Unlatch that critter."

I cannot tell you the solemn feeling I had, raising the lid of the chest. I looked inside and beheld some of the treasures of over a hundred years of life: A black leather family Bible, big and ornate, sealed with a tiny locked clasp. Infants' baptismal clothing. (It had never crossed my mind, till then, that Momma Opalona might really be a momma.) I placed aside a packet of letters, which had been secured with a pink ribbon, and colorless postcards with faded photographs. An open box of tintypes rattled in my hand, and scattered faces of folks who had lived a century ago stared at me with timeless eyes.

Soon as I saw it, I knew what it was: the diary. Momma Opalona's own momma's diary. It looked like a ledger book, but I knew it wasn't. I looked up at the old woman. She nodded, and I pulled the diary from its place of honor in her chest of treasures.

The three of us sat on the listening bench. Momma Opalona read from the diary: "This be the story of my three years with the Blood Peoples. By Winona Richardson. Written here by her own hand on April 4, 1877."

Momma Opalona ran her finger like a magic wand across the page, never touching the old brown ink, as she seemed to raise the words from the paper to her mouth by the power of her will:

"May 1865. They comes to me in a dream. My momma and poppa be dead, so I be living alone in the cabin, a girl of fourteen. They comes to me whilst I am dreaming. Only it ain't a dream. Just seems so. They send they children to fetch me. They takes me with them to they place on the mountain. Thus begins my captivity."

As Momma Opalona read, we became transformed by the revelation unfolding itself through the words of her mother. It was then I decided that one day I would tell this story, maybe even write it down "in my own hand." What a gift, I thought, to share with the ages—the gift Momma Opalona's momma had shared with us in her diary.

The diary explained that she was captured soon after she became an orphan at fourteen. I thought about Jule. She would appreciate that part of the story.

The woman said she wrote the diary some twelve years after the actual event. She said no one had believed her, so she decided to write it down in a diary, just in case. I appreciated that.

"On the full moon, they takes me to the top of the mountain. There, they puts pointed things into my arms and makes my blood to be they very own. It was then I becomes they slave. I knows what be happening. I just can't do nothing 'bout it. They tells me, in they mind, 'do this.' I do what they say. They says, 'do that.' I do that too."

Like Hannah Jane, John Croshaw, and the other children, I thought, *under a spell they cannot break.* I wanted to ask Momma Opalona to tell me how her mother got out, but I knew better. The old woman would tolerate no interruption.

I waited. I listened. I learned.

"Every year, thereabouts, they finds a new child to be they source of blood. Jus' one child. They only needs one. Times, I wonder, *Will they kill me?* But they don't. They lets me know in my mind they don't want to kill nobody. That be how they talks to me, in my mind. They lets me know in my mind they don't aims to kill me. They ain't killers. They just lost souls, abandoned by they own people, like so much garbage."

Like so much garbage. Momma Opalona had used those very words to us about the aliens. Were it not for Hannah Jane and the other kids, I would have felt sorry for the aliens. I knew what it was like to be alone and abandoned in those mountains.

Momma Opalona continued reading from the diary: "Every year, or thereabouts, they brings in a new child, but they don't do it on they own. They gets me, sometimes one of the others, to do they work for them."

So that's why they have so many children, I reflected. Every year they need fresh human blood. The blood from only one child. And John Croshaw? He too was under their spell, acting out their commands, capturing other children. That explained why he had tried so hard to dissuade me from coming along. They needed blood from only one child. I still didn't know why. The diary was no help there. It only told of the woman's experience. She didn't analyze it or try to give explanations for the blood ceremony. Perhaps she would not have even remembered it.

She did tell how she escaped:

"It be an accident. Otherwise, I be with them to this very day. It happens on the way to the mountaintop, to Devil's Head. I lines up behind one them Blood People and heads to Devil's Head. Somewhere on the way back, I slips and falls into a cove. Deep one. They searches for me. I knows that 'cause they tells me they is. I hears them in my mind, telling me I shouldn't ought to worry 'cause they gonna find me. But they don't. They be close, but old Mr. Sun start to come up, and they hightails it back to they cave. They say they come back next night for me—next night, they say, they finds me and takes me back with them. But I gets saved afore then."

Salvation came in the form of a former slave looking to make a home for himself in the mountains. He discovered the girl at the foot of the cliff. Found her, cut and bleeding, close to death from the fall. He nursed her back to health. He never once said she was as crazy as the story she told him sounded. They married.

"That man be my very own daddy," Momma Opalona said through a grin that now revealed two instead of three teeth. Before long, her smile faded. "I suppose you young'ns got you mind set to go on up there?" she said.

I didn't answer. But she knew what was in my mind, all the same.

I thanked her. The diary had not given us all we needed, but I figured it would be enough information to go from there. The hunter's moon would rise that evening. We decided to hide in the woods during the day, hoping to prepare some sort of plan that would work. I had not expected magic from Momma Opalona. Though, I was sorry none existed.

As we were about to leave her shack, she stopped me. "You take this with you," she said. She reached deeper into her trunk and pulled out a small tortoiseshell hand mirror. She said, "When I was growing up, my very own momma say I was never to go out on the full moon without it. But to be honest, I don't recall exactly why she imparted that piece of advice."

I took the mirror and packed it inside a blanket the woman insisted we take with us. I thanked her again, then I stepped out into the woods with the others. We set our sights on Devil's Mountain.

CHAPTER TWENTY-FOUR

A body can waste a passel of time
A-trying to put things in place,
While sometimes the explanation he seeks
Is plain as the nose on his face.

THE SUN HELD HIGH in the sky when we stopped to snack on the bread and hard salami Momma Opalona had given us for our journey. We had crossed the government-posted fence and Deadline Creek without incident. Devil's Head looked down upon us, smiling in the sunshine like a dangerous animal playing possum with a grin on its face. Devil's Mountain was deceptively harmless in the light of day. It was the light of the full moon that worried me.

We sat in a small clearing next to the stream I recognized from being lost there before. I had come back just about the same time of year. No snow this time. Made it more tolerable. I smelled the crispness of the autumn, though. There would be a cold wind blowing across the top of the mountain that night. This time, though, I had my bearings from the start. I knew where I was going and how to get back. What I did not know was what to do in between. We did our figuring while we ate.

"It's no mystery," Jule said. "Obvious as the nose on the end of your face." She acted like she understood it perfectly. "By mingling their blood with humans, the aliens receive some of our antibodies, allowing them to survive on Earth. But in doing so, the children who share blood with them receive some of the aliens' blood properties, which, it appears, keeps them passive and makes it possible for the aliens to communicate with them telepathically."

I looked at Gary Wayne. "Maybe she's one of them," I said.

Gary Wayne, as usual, believed Jule could do no wrong. "Just 'cause you don't understand it, don't mean she don't know what she's talking about."

"Hey, buddy," I said, "don't get your nose out of place. I'm just kidding. Course, you did see *I Married a Monster from Outer Space*, now, didn't you? I mean, it does make sense, you know, the way old Jule there seems to know all about—"

"You are out of line, now, I'm warning you." His finger probed dangerously close to my nose.

"Okay," I said, "maybe she ain't no monster from outer space. Hey, maybe *you're* the monster. You put that finger away. Might grow teeth, now. You know, like them lizard people out of the Black Lagoon."

Jule sighed. "Boys."

Gary Wayne said, "You are just jealous 'cause what she says makes sense."

To be honest, she did make sense. So I said, "I suppose that means, if the kidnapped children don't get a transfusion for a while, they return to normal human beings."

Jule nodded. "That's right, Chess."

I flashed Gary Wayne a now-who's-smart look.

Gary Wayne said, "So what we got to do is find a way to lead the kids away from the aliens long enough to break the spell. . . ."

"Long enough for the aliens' blood properties to lose their effectiveness in the human kids' bloodstream," Jule said.

Gary Wayne said, "That's what I meant."

Jule said, "Got any ideas how we should do this?" She looked straight at me, my mouth full of the sweet-tasting hard salami I always considered such a treat.

"I do have a plan," I said. "Only, it will take all of us to pull it off."

Gary Wayne said, "Go ahead, Chess."

I took a drink from the canteen we had brought from Mr. Duffy's cabin. "Here's the way I figure it, based on what I learned from my last visit to this place, and the diary of Momma Opalona's momma: First of all, I need to go down into their cave while they're gone, while they're on the way to Devil's Head for the ceremony. Remember I said they wore robes with hoods and all? Maybe one of us could pose as an alien wearing one of their robes, supposing they have an extra one lying around somewhere in the cave and I can find it down there. Maybe it's possible to lead the kids away, dressed like one of the aliens."

Jule interrupted. "What robes with hoods and all? Chess, you sure you're not getting these fellows confused with some other organization?"

I said, "Very funny, Jule, but I do know the difference. The aliens' robes were shiny-like, sort of reflected the light of the moon."

"Like shields?" she asked.

That girl bothered me. She never said much, but when she did, it always made sense.

"Yeah," I said, a light going on in my head. Why hadn't I thought of that? "Yeah, they did keep those things on till the actual blood ceremony. Then they dropped their robes like they were allowing the full force of the moon's rays against their bodies."

Jule said, "That means they must be hypersensitive to moonlight, any kind of light for that matter. Fresh human blood in their bodies probably allows them some moments of safe exposure to the forces of light, moonlight in this case."

Gary Wayne laughed. "I been meaning to point that out to you, Chess."

"Sure, Gary Wayne, just sort of slipped your mind, I suppose." I looked at Jule, thinking that all that happens to a body happens for a purpose. Had it not been for the death of her grandfather, she would not have been along to help us interpret the events to follow.

She had a pensive look on her face. "That's it!" she said. "They get energy from moonlight, just like plants and animals get energy from the sun. We'd get sick, maybe die without sunrays, you know."

Gary Wayne looked at me again, proud as a new father. "I been meaning to explain that one to you, too, Chess."

Thinking it over, the logic was undeniable. Those people, whoever they were, were aliens to our planet. But they still needed light energy to survive, like all life forms do. Only, their bodies couldn't tolerate the intensity of light even from our moon. Momma Opalona was right. The sun would make them shrivel up and die.

It was the properties in our blood, allowing them the few moments of immunity to the moonlight, which gave them time to recharge their batteries, so to speak. Jule was a genius. Not that I would have admitted it to her.

Rubbing my fingers up and down my chin, I did concede, "Jule, you may be onto something there."

Of course, what it was, I couldn't explain at the time. But it did give us an angle we needed to devise our plan for rescuing Hannah Jane and the rest of the kidnapped children.

Our discussions did not proceed without argument. I decided I wanted to go down to the cave, once the aliens and children had passed us on the trail leading up to Devil's Head.

Gary Wayne didn't think that was such a great idea. "Are you crazy, Chester?" He waited for an answer that did not come. "You really are crazy. Hey, pal, this ain't Joe Ray McQuarter you're aiming to run into. One thing to stand up for yourself, but this . . . this . . . this idea is just plain crazy."

I tried to explain, to tell him how I needed to know more about them, maybe even discover some children down there.

He saw no wisdom in my plan. None at all. "It's crazy, Chess. All you're gonna do is get yourself trapped, and then they'll go after me and Jule. Don't you see?"

I did see. I saw how dumb and dangerous it all sounded. But I also saw that we had nothing to hang our hopes on. I saw that I had to go down there to find a way out or. . . .

I really tried to keep the "or" out of my thoughts.

Jule said, "Chester, I find that I have to agree with Gary Wayne. One would suppose your plan foolhardy. Now, we are not saying that we don't appreciate your intentions."

Something in the back of my mind told me I had to enter that cave. Maybe it was the guilt I felt for having run away when I was first on the mountain. I had followed them to their hideaway. But I went no farther, leaving to others the job of bringing them out of captivity. My fear haunted me. I would have to face it. And, in doing so, I prayed I would find a way to free the children.

"I'm going down there," I said. I said it in a way that they both understood my meaning. "You can help me, or you can take off. I won't hold it against you, Gary Wayne." I looked at Jule. "Maybe you ought to go, either way," I said.

The looks on their faces told me they would stay. They were not happy about my plan, but they would stay, as Gary Wayne said, "So as to bail you out when the aliens get their hands on you." I really hoped that would not be necessary.

We did agree that Jule and Gary Wayne would act as lookouts. They were to signal me if any of the aliens came back. We hadn't figured out just how they would do that, though. We also hadn't figured what to do if I found nothing down in that cave but cold air. To my everlasting embarrassment, I let it slip out that I did have an idea that there might be "some kind of ray guns down there or something I could use as weapons against the creatures."

Gary Wayne rolled his eyes at Jule, who shrugged and said, "Ray gun, Chester? I do hope you will not take offense if I mention that ray guns are a picture-show invention. I mean, Flash Gordon did have access to ray guns, but they were not real. You see, in the movies there are people who make things called props, and—"

"Okay, Jule, don't rub it in. All I know for sure is that we don't know anything for sure. So I'm going down into that cave to see what I can find out. That's the first part of our plan. The rest, we piece together as we go along. Now, let's get ready."

First we took stock of what we had with us. Momma Opalona had directed us to the homes of several of her friends, with orders to supply our needs, "no questions asked." We made good use of their kindness.

We had learned a lesson looking for Mr. Mullins without preparation. This time we took with us about fifty feet of cotton rope and an old miner's coal-oil lamp, which Jule wore on her head. She put food in her knapsack along with more practical things like a couple of novels and the personal grooming equipment Gary Wayne and I hadn't learned the necessity of yet. I pulled out Momma Opalona's mirror and put it in my jacket pocket. I wondered about that.

I had seen in the picture shows that vampires don't like to look at themselves in mirrors. That's what Dracula's cloak was about—mirrors. And the sun, of course. In the movies, whenever he happened upon a mirror, he would swish his cape over his eyes. I decided that would be too simple an explanation. Somehow, I didn't think that was the purpose of the little vanity mirror Momma Opalona had given me.

It was getting on toward evening, and the temperature dropped enough that all of us put on our coats. Gary Wayne had brought kitchen matches, a bowie knife, and line and tackle for fishing. I carried a small bow saw, for cutting dead firewood, and a collapsible army shovel to make a latrine and cover our fire, should we need one.

Each of us had a sleeping bag and food. This time, I felt I had come to the mountain prepared. I just wasn't sure if the aliens would cooperate.

CHAPTER TWENTY-FIVE

To catch a critter
Lay a noose.
Lay it lazy, lay it loose.
Spring the trap
When all is right,
Right to hold the critter tight.
And never, never, never let
The critter trap you
In your net.

SOMETIMES EVENTS PASS BY YOU SO FAST, they seem to happen as if in a dream. And when you try to recollect them, you wonder, *Is this the way it happened?* This is how I remember what happened next. It all comes back to me as if it were happening now:

The hair on the back of my neck stands straight up. I can almost feel the heat from his body, the way he gains on me as I scamper through the trees, scant yards ahead of him at most. A part of me feels almost grateful. He has been on my trail since I left Devil's Mountain to report how he had tricked Hannah Jane and me into doing something stupid. I had seen him all those other times. In the alley. On a road leading to the reformatory. Somehow, he had managed to find a way into the prison—and a way out. He had outsmarted the men and dogs chasing Gary Wayne and me through the woods. He had discovered our resting place at Mr. Duffy's cabin, and he even followed us to Momma Opalona's. Only, the Melungeon hermit, Denny Mullins, had outsmarted him—for a time. And now, I am figuring on doing the same thing.

But he has a different idea.

I am running full-out now, my lungs working hard, an ache growing in my legs. My muscles had started to burn long ago, when he first sensed that I was alone and vulnerable. It took him a time to catch up, but now he is on top of me. I have one more trick to play. I lunge to the left as he reaches for the back of my shirt. I can hear him crashing into the trees.

More distance. I must put more distance between him and me. Uphill. The ground suddenly closes to my face. Arms working as hard as legs, pulling at anything that will help me to the top of just one more ridge. My legs scream now, and my lungs start to give up. Almost to the top. He is behind me again, his lungs working like bellows. I reach for the top, try to pull myself over. Downhill soon. Downhill, I can recover. Almost there. Another yard.

No, I feel his hand on my shirt, pulling me back, pulling against my resistance. The grass slipping my grip. Now the dirt. Now nothing. I am falling backwards. He is beside me. Two formless bodies tumbling over and over, down and down. We crash at the bottom. No one moves. I try to rise and give up, let go, will run no more. Beside me, his breathing increases. He rises and stands over me.

I hear my voice and repeat Hannah Jane's plea: "Why are you doing this to me?"

The dream faded when he caught me.

I could see things clearer.

I could see how it all went wrong, when I miscalculated my own speed and agreed to meet with Gary Wayne and Jule at the edge of a clearing, one ridge over from where I now lay, wasted from a chase that had started almost half an hour earlier.

I could see him as a person now, not a monster who had been chasing me for such a long time.

He said, "Get up."

"You'll have to carry me out of here," I told him.

"Then, I'll carry you." He reached down and struggled to lift me from the damp ground, now partly covered with fresh snow. A wet snow.

I had grown since he last saw me. My clothes were wet. He would have to work to get me back to the aliens. But he knew his own tricks and jabbed a thumb under my chin, pushing it deeper into my throat, until I had to stand for the pain.

He pointed up a ridge in the other direction from which we had just fallen. "That way," he said. "You try to run, I'll just catch you again."

I decided to try reasoning with him. "Hey, John, you don't have to do this. I remember you from school."

He ignored me. I turned to face him, but he pushed me around.

"Keep moving."

I pulled my arm away and said, "Hey, you ain't stupid are you? Are you stupid? Come on, this is really crazy."

"I will hurt you." The look on his face told me he meant it, but it wasn't a look of meanness or anger. It was almost no look, a kind of nothingness to his expression that scared me more than any threat or punishment he would mete out.

I started up the ridge. In the back of my mind, I was not yet ready to fight. When I caught my breath, then I would fight if I had to fight.

At the top, he pointed down a deer trail. The longer we followed the trail, the more I realized that no wild animal had used this pathway in a long time.

"We'll wait here," he finally said. Then he said something to himself, something that made sense only when I recalled Momma Opalona's mother's diary. The part about how they spoke to her without words, like sending a message from one mind to another. His words confirmed that to me: "Must wait till they know I'm here."

I said, "Did you hear what you just said?"

A look came to his eyes. Confusion. He was following orders, all right. But he was not in contact with them, not yet. John Croshaw, the boy I hated out of jealousy, was waiting for orders. Everything he had done up to that time was under the control of those beings who hid on top of that mountain. I hated him no more.

"Listen to me," I said. "Those . . . those aliens, they're telling you to do bad things. I mean, John, this ain't the real you. Can you understand what I'm saying?"

He stared, nothing happening in his eyes. For a moment, I thought I saw the confusion again. I wondered about the power they could have over us. In school, he had acted normal—arrogant, yes; too good to be true, for sure—but normal. But now?

He rose, and his head jerked, first one way, then the other. He seemed to understand what was happening.

Gary Wayne came up behind him. Jule took up her position closer to me. We had him from three directions.

I said, "If you run, John Croshaw, we will catch you."

He started to his right. I cut him off, just as Gary Wayne slammed into him, a perfect tackle, arms wrapped around the boy's waist as he took him all the way to the ground.

Jule knelt in front him. "We won't hurt you," she whispered. Her hand stroked his head where he had bruised it against the ground.

"We will pick you up on the way back, okay?"

The boy's face remained in neutral, showing neither fear nor anger. The ropes cut deep into his arms and wrists, and I winced at how securely Gary Wayne had hog-tied the boy who had been on our trail for so long.

"He'll be okay," Gary Wayne said. "Ropes won't cut off his circulation, lessen he tries to escape."

Jule put one of our blankets over him.

The funny part was how resigned John Croshaw seemed to the captivity in which we had placed him.

Gary Wayne leaned over to him and said, "Don't you go nowhere, now." He then rose and looked at me. "Well, Chess, it didn't work out exactly the way we planned it, but we got him, all the same." When I hadn't made it to the designated location for the ambush, the two of them had to run to take up the slack I'd lost.

I collapsed to the ground, exhausted, and we had only accomplished the easy part. Now all we had to do was deal with the vampire aliens.

CHAPTER TWENTY-SIX

In the deep, deep dark
Hear the wolf dog bark,
Or maybe a monster or so,
Waiting quietly for me
In the dark where I can't see.
Through the silent, deadly passages I go.

IT STARTED TO SNOW HEAVIER. Possibly, the moon would be obscured by clouds and the ceremony would have to be postponed. We waited, hidden above the great rock where I had followed the children and their alien captors a year ago. It was past midnight. From our concealed position, we saw the trail that led up to Devil's Head.

By three in the morning, I had fallen asleep. I awoke to see them standing over me.

The one who seemed to be in charge pointed at me. I didn't hear a word, but I knew what it said to the others: "Take that one. He knows too much."

I started to scream for Gary Wayne, but the alien who had grabbed me put his fingerless hand over my mouth. I couldn't breathe. All of a sudden, I felt as if I would die. I fought to pull his hand from my mouth, but he wouldn't budge. He kept pressing against me, tighter, tighter, tighter still.

So this is what it feels like to die, I thought.

After a while I stopped struggling. It didn't hurt so much anymore. I felt myself at peace and said, "Okay, Chester, it's your time. Don't fight it. It's time for the new adventure. Let go."

I did. That's when I woke up with Gary Wayne's hand over my mouth.

"They're leaving the cave now," he said. "I thought you were going to break free and start screaming and give us away for sure."

We waited as the aliens herded their captives away from the

cave. I had been able to see only the tail end of the children being led up to Devil's Head. If my memory served me right, it would take them over half an hour to reach the meadow where they had their ceremony. The ceremony itself lasted only a few minutes, so I said to Jule and Gary Wayne, "I got to be in and out of there in forty-five minutes."

We had figured out a way of signaling me if there was trouble, and it would also keep me from getting lost while I was looking for a spare robe down in the cave. I tied the end of Gary Wayne's fishing line to my wrist.

"If I pull on the line three times, that means I need to get out in a hurry," I explained to them.

Jule said, "Same warning out here. We pull on it three times, you get on out, but make sure you watch your step." She didn't have to tell me that if they pulled on that string, my chances of getting out of the cave were slim and none.

The first thirty yards or so were easy enough, if you like walking around in a dark cave. I wore the coal-oil miner's lamp. It lighted my way a few yards, no more. I also knew it made me an easy target if one of them stood guard in there somewhere.

By a hundred yards, I was lost and praying the fishing line didn't get cut on a sharp rock. I heard sounds like animals baying, then I realized the wind whistled and gusted through the cave as I descended. An underground stream bubbled like a brook. The air got colder. My footsteps echoed down the passageway as I stepped into an enormous opening. Even my breathing seemed to bounce against the cathedral-like walls. I looked up and saw nothing but darkness.

From the light of my dim lantern, it looked to me that the cavern was almost the size of a football field, with the stream cutting through it down the center. I discovered smaller caves on the sides. I thought of cells in a prison. But these prisoners were put there from another planet.

The urge to pull on the string and get out of there was so strong that I tugged on it once, then again. I stopped myself. *Remember, Chess, you may fail, but you got a reason to step out onto that field of battle.*

I walked toward the first cave. Empty.

The next, also.

At the third cave, a larger one, I pulled up. On the ground, in the fine chalky dust, were footprints, many footprints. I walked into the cavern to investigate.

A whisper escaped my lips: "This must be where they sleep." It was clear to anyone experienced at looking for places where animals bedded down. The ground was worn, pushed aside, dug out like an animal does where it sleeps. Especially an animal who had slept in one place for a hundred years. No trace of food. No scraps. No garbage. Not even a waste heap. Then I remembered how John Croshaw never ate. He drank—drank greedily—but I never saw him eat food.

Something behind me got my attention. I turned with a jerk, looking at the mouth of the cave I had just entered. I saw nothing. My eyes blinked. A light? Something caught my eye. I wasn't sure what it was.

"There it is again!" I whispered.

A sound? No, it wasn't noise. My senses were on edge. I hadn't heard anything, but I sensed another presence. The hairs on the back of my neck stood at attention. Someone was down there with me in that dark cavern.

I crept to the opening of the cave where I decided the children must have slept, and peeked around the mouth. Again I saw nothing, heard nothing. Nothing but the bubbling of the stream.

"Is that it?" I asked myself. "Is it the stream?" I wanted to laugh but decided against any unnecessary noise. "You're talking to yourself, Chess. First sign of losing it."

That's when I saw a flicker of light outside in the darkness of the cavern. I blew out my lamp and stayed quiet, looking for a light I was sure I had seen, listening for someone, waiting for that someone to come in my direction. For a while, I saw nothing, heard nothing. Nothing but the stream.

I was about to reach into my pocket and pull out a match to relight the lamp, when I saw it again. A flicker of light, then it was gone. This time, there was no doubt. Someone was with me. I felt my way around the wall of the cave. I saw it again.

For sure, this time I had seen a light, dimmer even than the lamp I had just snuffed out. It flickered from another small cave, near forty yards up from where I was. Something drew me toward the light. I had to see what was in there. I prayed that whoever it was hadn't seen me as well.

Every step I took sounded like someone had slammed a door. I hoped the rippling of the stream would cover me as I worked my way toward the source of the light in the cave. Within ten yards, I heard something again. I started to turn and had it in my mind to tiptoe away as fast as I could without making any noise. I made it only a quarter way around, when the alien stepped out into the large cavern and came toward me.

I was so startled, I froze. Had it read my presence? I tried to move, but I was so scared I couldn't. An idea came to me to press against the wall, to flatten my body into the crevices that angled up the walls like deep grains in a tree trunk.

But the alien came straight at me, and the closer he came, the more paralyzed I became. He was almost on top of me. The light from his body reflected against mine. So the source of the light was the alien himself . . . or herself. Itself? Whatever, I waited helplessly, trying not to imagine what he would do to me. But he did nothing. He walked right on by, as if I were somehow invisible to him.

For a reason I could not fathom, he hadn't seen me. But I did see him. Saw him clearly. He passed me close enough, I could have reached out and touched him. The thought sent a shiver down my spine. In the dark there, he wore no robe, no hood over his face. The light I had seen come from him looked pale yellow, tinges of green on the edges, almost neon, revealing features I previously thought did not exist when I first had seen the aliens from a distance. I saw those features now, illuminated by the alien's own body light. It was as if I could see into the creature itself.

He walked effortlessly, silently, across the floor of the cave, looking as light as air. He did have fingers, if you could call them that. They were more like gills that closed against the hand. I saw the lines between them, though they were folded and streamlined when not in use. Tiny holes opened into his head—front, sides, and back. I couldn't decide if they were ears or breathing holes—or both. But they served a purpose—I supposed.

Eyes? No, he didn't have eyes. He had an eye—one eye—suspended in the middle of his head. I mean in the *middle*, right there in the center of his transparent head was this eyeball that seemed to just float there like a fish in a fishbowl. The eye seemed to have hundreds of facets, like an insect's, so it could see in every direction at once, or focus all its power in one direction. It seemed to go back and forth, focusing straight ahead, then all around, depending on the direction the creature took. That part felt the eeriest to me, watching him walk away from me with an eye in the center of his head so he could see where he had been as well as where he was going. That's when I figured out why he hadn't seen me. Movement. I had learned in biology class that insects' eyes focus on movement. I stayed still, tried hard not even to breathe.

In a few moments, he faded from sight, like he had walked into the stone. Only, I knew he entered another cave, because I saw the dim light reflect shadows momentarily, then they were gone. Why was he there and not with the others? My curiosity took me toward the place he had been.

I groped along the wall of the cave, feeling for the entrance to the cave he had left. I couldn't risk relighting my lamp, so I felt around in the dark, listening for any sound that would tell me danger was near. There was nothing. I found the opening and moved into the cave, waving my hands in front of me, feeling here and there, hoping I wouldn't find something I didn't want to find.

The darkness sapped my energy. I felt like a swimmer in the ocean, not knowing what monster might be closing in on the parts of my body I couldn't see.

All of a sudden, I stopped worrying that I might run into something I didn't need to find. I found it. I touched something that made my heart stop.

Unlike the cool walls of the cave or the brittle, sandy ground, this felt soft and ice cold. Soon as I touched it, a faint light, dimmer than the other creature's, flickered from what I touched. It came from an alien lying on the ground, looking more dead than alive. He lay situated in a corner, on a cot of some kind. From the dim light he emitted, I could make out a tube connected to his body at the arm. I knew the purpose of that tube, anyway.

He must be sick, I decided, waiting for the others to return, waiting for fresh blood. And the other creature must be attending to him. I let my eyes adjust to the light. On the other side of this sleeping alien, a robe lay neatly folded. Not used for the cold. The creature had felt icy cold to me. No, the robe provided protection from something else. My mind started to run wild. I had stumbled onto more than a sick alien. The creature moved, almost a twitch. I had to get out of there before his friend returned.

Time crawls when you're afraid and in a hurry. I could not run or risk waking the sick creature. In the back of my mind, I could see the other one looking at me face to face when I exited the cave. Almost at the mouth of the cave, I stopped. The robe. It's what I came for, and I almost left without it. A plan had formed in my mind. I turned around and crept again toward the alien.

I stood over him, reminding myself why I had come back. He still seemed unconscious. A film covered his eye, which reassured me he was still asleep. Soundly, I hoped.

My attention focused on the robe. *Now's your chance, Chess. Reach over and get it. That robe is going to work magic for you tonight.* Problem was, the robe lay on the other side of a sleeping alien, and the only way to get it was to reach over the creature and take it.

I moved like a snail. Down on my knees. Every second, I imagined the other one coming up behind me. I forced myself to block out the image and focus on the task at hand.

Not easy. I had already tried to step over the alien to get the robe. It wouldn't work; I chanced stomping the creature. Not a good idea. *That's all you need, Chess,* I told myself. *Probably squash him, and then see who gets mad.* There was only one way—on hands and knees.

I took my position, balancing my left hand across the body of the alien while I reached for the robe with my right. This would work, I tried to convince myself. Except. Always an except. In this instance, the distance between the robe and the alien was so far, I had to place my face almost directly over his face to reach the robe. I tried not to breathe when I did so. *There.*

I took hold of it, tried to gather it in my hand. Heavier than it looked, much heavier. I had to move carefully so that none of the fabric would touch the alien. No going back. I had to lift my prize slowly across his sleeping body. A cold sweat had broken out all over me, and drops began to roll down my face and onto the alien.

Oh, Chester, your luck, and that thing will open its eye sure as you're halfway over.

I was wrong. He did not open his eye when I was halfway over; he opened it soon as I started to lift the robe.

I screamed. Instinctively, I let out a scream—and for good reason. His eye, big as a tennis ball, looked straight into mine, and I screamed like it was the last thing I was going to do on this earth, and I wanted to make it last. I was halfway down the side of the big cave before I had enough sense to realize that I still had the robe in my hand. At least I got that part right. But my problems weren't over.

Directly in front of me, blocking my escape from the great cavern, stood the other alien. And he wasn't sick.

CHAPTER TWENTY-SEVEN

In the dim dark of the night
When the creature stands in fright,
Who's to know what's wrong or right?
Time to stop and strike a light.

"OKAY, CHESS," I said. "You been discovered. May as well light up that old lamp and get a good look at him getting a good look at you."

Thwickkkkkkktsssss! Soon as I drew the kitchen match across the sole of my boot, that creature threw up its hands in front of its face and seemed to glide into the nearest cave like a ghost slipping into its own grave. I got the idea. Self-preservation makes a body resourceful in a hurry. Holding the lighted lamp out in front of me like a hunter with a gun, I pulled three times on the fishing line and followed the gentle tug of my lifeline out of the cave.

Jule and Gary Wayne looked at me like they had seen a ghost. They almost had.

I said, "I ran into two of them in there, one sick, the other caring for him. When I struck a match to light the lamp, it chased away the one who meant to stop me."

Then the thought struck me. "We best hurry," I said. "I'm betting the aliens I ran into in that cave have already relayed the information to their friends."

We headed out on the trail. As we hiked, I explained what I thought we would have to do. "I got real lucky," I said to them. "They don't like light of any kind. We can use the lamp against them."

Jule and Gary Wayne seemed to get the idea. "So we distract them with the lamp," Gary Wayne said.

"While one of us, wearing this robe, leads the children away," Jule added.

I was impressed but didn't let on. "Yeah, Jule, something like that. We use this cape to fool the kids into following one of us. The trick is to find a way to get them moving in that direction without the creatures objecting."

"We can use the lamp to blind the . . . you know, the aliens or whatever they are," Gary Wayne pointed out.

"But I suspect we'll need more than this lamp," I said. "Separating the children from the aliens may take a little more encouraging than scaring them with light and one of us wearing this robe."

Gary Wayne asked, "What you got in mind, Chess?"

"We need to corral them," I said, "like sheep. They acted just like sheep the last I saw them. You still got some of that rope left over, Gary Wayne?"

He smiled. Gary Wayne was quick to adapt to a plan.

While he looked for someplace to secure the rope, I took the small shovel and started to dig a channel across the trail. I figured we had twenty minutes, assuming the aliens in the cave had warned the others. I looked up. The snow had stopped. But the clouds remained. If the clouds parted, the moon would be at its brightest. It was another hunter's moon. Tonight, the aliens were the hunters. Jule, Gary Wayne, and I were the game.

We worked extra hard. Gary Wayne had finished his work with the rope. I handed him the bow saw. "Maybe a couple of trees?" I said.

Gary Wayne understood. "Maybe we could even the odds a little," he said.

We worked like scared kids. And because we were scared, we worked hard. Jule piled up handfuls of dry leaves. The trench I had dug across a narrow part of the trail was about three feet deep. Gary Wayne had finished notching three small beech trees and helped me shovel, using his own two hands, throwing rock and dirt aside like a mole looking to get into the safety of its hole.

"Bring up some broken tree branches," I said to Jule. She laid them across the trench, which was just wide enough for us to spread an open sleeping bag across and cover it with dead leaves.

I said, "The last time they came along this trail, they didn't seem to be afraid of anything. I hope they're as confident this time."

We were to find out soon. I heard the first faint footsteps coming up the mountain. We got out of sight on the high side of the trail.

I explained, "When I followed them last year, one of the aliens led the children, while the others lagged behind making sure no one strayed off the trail. Every now and then, they had to herd any stragglers. After Momma Opalona's momma dropped off, I suppose they learned their lesson. Now, here's what we do. . . ."

Gary Wayne had crossed over and waited on the low side of the trail they would be taking back from Devil's Head. He wore the alien's robe. Directly across from him, lying on her stomach, covered by ground fern, hid Jule, her hand firmly gripping one side of the rope. Gary Wayne had tied the other side to a balsam tree almost fifty feet down the trail, and I waited there.

In my right hand I held a match. The other held onto the lamp. I just hoped it lighted on the first try. I had only one other match, just in case. I held my breath. So far, everything went as I had planned. The lead alien appeared over the crest of the trail, some thirty yards below me. They would be distracted, I figured. Our presence would have interrupted their blood ceremony. So far, the cloud cover held. They would not have had time for their ceremony. I also deduced they would probably want to capture us and include us in their ceremony if our plan failed.

Been here before, I thought. Only, it wasn't the mountain.

It was down at the reformatory, waiting in a cold latrine, getting ready to make a break for my freedom. My stomach sank, and the old bugs returned with a vengeance. I had to force myself to forget about the fact that almost everything had gone wrong with our plans that night. I didn't have to force myself long. In a few seconds they would be upon us. I wouldn't have to worry about whether or not our plans would or wouldn't work. I'd know for sure.

The lead alien passed by me, walking as effortlessly as the one I had seen in the cave. The children passed, one by one: The little girl who had led me and the posse astray. The Cherokee children. Another kid with a stupid look on his face, every bit as much under control as the others. Suddenly, a black boy my age, a blank stare in his eyes, stumbled and fell in my direction, almost stepping right on top of me. He was close enough that I looked into his blank brown eyes.

Oh, no, he's going to give me away. But he didn't. He didn't even blink. Just pulled himself upright and continued on the trail.

They were almost past me, halfway to the next stage of our plan. I saw the other aliens lagging behind. I readied my match. Then something happened that dropped the blood in my body down to my feet. Hannah Jane walked by.

She walked at the end of the line. She looked the same as she had looked the last time I saw her. She seemed to stare at me from out of her vacant eyes. I wanted to reach out and touch her, pull her to me, and take off, carrying her safely down the mountain. I forgot where I was and what I had planned to do. It all hinged on me, the whole plan, and I was paralyzed by the sight of Hannah Jane, seeming to scream silently for me to help her. I almost did, too. I almost reached out for her. Would have, I suppose, if it hadn't been for the ruckus breaking out up the trail.

The lead alien fell into the trench like a trapped animal.

Jule jumped from her hiding place, ran across the path in front of the trench, pulling the rope with her, using it to herd the children in the direction of Gary Wayne, dressed like an alien, who calmly walked down the side of the mountain, cutting through the trees with the kids following meekly behind him.

By that time, I had collected myself and started the first part of my plan: pushing the beech trees, which Gary Wayne had notched, over the path, separating the aliens from the kids. Then I pulled the match across the fallen log nearest me. The match broke off. I had pulled too hard. The next one lighted. By the time I got the lamp lit, the aliens were cowering on the ground, shielding their faces and bodies from the light. I watched the last of the kids, including Hannah Jane, trail down the side of the hill, with Gary Wayne in the lead and Jule herding along behind. They had reached the end of their rope, but by then, the children had honed in on Gary Wayne like chicks to a mother hen.

"Keep going!" I yelled to them. "It's working just like we planned. Soon as it gets light, I'll meet you down the mountain."

In a few minutes, I couldn't hear them anymore. The only sound was the rustling of the aliens' robes as they tried to burrow into the ground against the light of the lamp. I looked back up the trail just in time to see the one in the trench peek his head over the edge, then duck down again.

"He won't be a problem," I whispered.

I looked at the sky. It was clear now. I wondered what would happen to the aliens now that they would not get their fresh blood. I wondered who had been their victim that night. Who had led the child into the trap? A part of me felt sorry for the aliens. I was sure the recently captured child was now thanking Gary Wayne and Jule for what they did to save all the kids, and was telling them how it would be neat to brag about it to others, and how the night would be an adventure to remember—which it was indeed. I thought of the aliens, felt sorry for them.

"Just trying to survive," I spoke out loud, almost like I was having a friendly conversation with myself.

I did not feel afraid. That surprised me. I had stepped out onto that field of battle scared to death. And now the battle seemed over, and I did not feel afraid anymore. "Another hour," I said, estimating the time till dawn. Should I go before then, I wondered, and give the aliens the chance to get back into their cave?

A part of me said, *Yes.* But a dark part of me said, *No! No, Chester, the sheriff won't believe you again.* That's when it struck me: *Of course, he'll believe you. Hannah Jane and John Croshaw will be safe and alive. The other kids, including the one just captured. They will tell. The law will have to believe you.* I took a deep breath, cleaning the confusion from my tired mind.

"I can't kill you," I said to them, "no more than you could deliberately kill those children you kept hostage all these years."

I stood up from the birch log on which I'd been resting and started down the trail. "It's over," I said to the aliens.

Then something happened that made me say, "No, it ain't!"

CHAPTER TWENTY-EIGHT

When all is lost
Or seems to be,
It's time to make a bet
That till the lights
Are all turned out,
The game ain't over yet.

A COAL-OIL LAMP does take a long time to dim and then go out. It flickers a time or two, then total darkness. I was surrounded immediately—by darkness and the aliens.

I took a deep breath and let it out slowly. "Well," I said, "maybe you're going to get your yearly dose of human blood, after all." It seemed that was their intention.

They did not handle me roughly. Their hands were cold and kept me securely in their grasp, but they were not hard on me.

I had gone numb by the time they put me down in the middle of the open meadow on Devil's Head. My friends could not come to my aid in time. I knew that. Would they come at all? I could only hope so. But that wasn't my immediate concern.

A cold wind blew across my face. I tried to feel it as long as I could. I concentrated on feeling, hoping it would somehow fix a memory in my mind, a memory that might make me realize that no matter what happened, I'm still human.

They were in the process of forming their circle. Feathery clouds blew slowly across the moon and started to dissipate. The aliens waited, looking up at the moon like they had done when I watched them with Hannah Jane. I tried not to think about it. Instead, I concentrated on my own senses.

Fix the memories, I told myself. *Look at the trees, Chess. Remember your daddy and you walking these woods. Smell the grass, the dirt under your body, hot bread and jam, your mother's toilet water, the smell of a new baby, a puppy dog kissing your face like you're its momma. Touch the ground, feel its hard texture against your stomach when you watch the water bugs play in the cold stream. See yourself, Chess. Picture what you look like. Don't let them make you forget who you are, what you look like . . . what you look like . . . what you look. . . .*

The mirror. Momma Opalona's mirror.

The cloud drifted away from the moon. One of my captors reached down and inserted a needle into a vein of my arm. John Croshaw had lied. It did hurt. It hurt like fire. But I forced myself to relax. That's when they started purring again. I felt it vibrate through my body. It wasn't scary. Fact is, I felt like going to sleep, and I had to fight to concentrate on keeping conscious.

One of them still held me. The other had released his grip, readying himself to push the needle up under my other arm when the time came. I watched the others pass the tube between them. The blood began to flow from my body into theirs. I saw it go from one to the other, their robes now down from their bodies, which were beginning to glow transparently, their blood vessels showing through the milky skin.

The children seemed indifferent to what was happening. It came to me, *You will soon be just like them, Chess.*

The blood had reached the middle alien and was now flowing back toward me. The alien who held me tightened his grip with one hand and freed his other arm, which he raised so the alien next to him could insert the needle and complete the next-to-last link of the circle. In a few seconds, my own blood, mixed with the aliens' blood, would return to me.

I prayed for a miracle and thought of the mirror. It was in my right-hand coat pocket. Only my left arm was free. I tried not to tip them off as I reached slowly across my body for the pocket. The alien next to me became distracted, having the needle inserted into his arm. Except for me, the circle was complete. He reached for me just as I drew the mirror from my pocket and held it to his face.

Nothing happened. The alien did not react to the mirror. *Good try, Chess. Vampires are not afraid of their own reflections.*

I didn't want to fight anymore. The alien next to me fumbled with the needle. He didn't even look at the mirror in my hand. Obviously not important to him.

Let go, I said to myself as I raised my arm, hoping the needle would go easier into this side than the other side. I looked at the moon. It was the last thing I would see as a human. It held my attention as I tried not to look down at the needle which I felt against my skin. A flicker of moonlight reflected across the face of the mirror, like the sun off a car window, making me blink. That's when I figured out what Momma Opalona had forgotten.

The reflection from the mirror.

The aliens could not look into light, any light, not even moonlight. But, with a mirror, they could be fooled. I felt the needle burn into my skin. I watched the blood flow into the last alien, heading in my direction. And I waved the mirror at the moon like crazy.

One of the aliens jumped, and they all did. The moon's reflection from the mirror flashed across his skin and hissed and singed like the flash from a burned-out lightbulb. I freed up my right hand and pulled the needle from my arm just as the first drops of blood trickled out the end, dripping harmlessly to the ground.

I was atop the crest of Devil's Head before the aliens recovered. They had their fix of fresh blood. I discovered they were not going to be grateful enough for my contribution to let me go without a chase.

It was on. I scrambled across the rocks and gravel, just like Hannah Jane and John Croshaw had done a year ago, clawing and sliding my way down, falling and recovering my balance, trying to keep ahead of the aliens. Every now and then, I stopped and flashed the mirror, and they ducked to cover themselves with their robes. I was losing ground, weak from loss of blood.

When I reached the trees, and it was too dark to find the moon, they had the advantage. In the clearings, I could flash the mirror again. It slowed them, but it didn't stop them.

Then I stumbled over a fallen log. I fell flat on my face and watched the mirror fly from my hands down a small cove.

By the time I caught my breath, it was too late. They had gathered around me. One of the aliens reached toward me. I could tell from the way he touched me, he still wasn't angry. But I pulled away and fell head-over-heels down the cove. I found the mirror. Broken into a thousand pieces.

"Chester," I said, "the battle is over, and you lost."

I was too tired to run. Three of them headed down the small cove toward me. I wondered if I still had any energy left in me to put up a fight.

I wouldn't have to.

The three aliens suddenly turned and ran back up the hill. They followed the others, who had hightailed it up the mountain like deer during hunting season.

I couldn't figure it out. I looked down at the mirror. It was truly busted. They did not fear me. Of that I was a-certain. I sat there for almost five minutes, too exhausted to do anything else.

Finally, I collected what little strength I had left and stood up. That's when I saw it, standing there next to me, pretty as a flower rising from the ground in springtime.

My shadow!

The sun's yellow smile sparkled over the eastern side of the mountains. I was saved.

EPILOGUE

Swing softly 'cross the chords of childhood past
To touch the tales and fantasies that last
Beyond dimensions grownups recognize
And fill their fancy in the children's eyes.

Hum the tunes that tinker in your mind
Inside that magic world where you will find
The stories you once longed at night to hear
When, snuggled in the warmth of playmates near,
You touched the stars that twinkled in your mind.

THE SHERIFF did believe me. The Army and Air Force believed me, too. They had, in fact, known of the aliens' presence for some time, but because of bureaucratic confusion, and their fear that the public would discover the truth of the legend, they chose to do nothing more than put a fence around the site. Now that the story was out, they moved a special mobile camp into the area and increased the security around a new fence they constructed in place of the old one. The new fence is now electrified and off limits, to this day. Rumor has it that they have made some kind of contact with the aliens—even to providing fresh human blood for them each year—but they won't deny or confirm it.

Publicly, the authorities—whoever they may be—had made it known that the presence of so many children, all of a sudden liberated from captivities of varying lengths, was in reality the result of some kind of government experiment gone awry, and certainly not the result of alien invasion. That did not stop public interest, nor the invasion of bureaucrats.

Another army—anthropologists, psychologists, biologists, social scientists, nuclear scientists, rocket scientists, and just about every other person with an "ist" to his or her name—moved into the area to work with the children who had been kidnapped. Many of them are still around, though they have been educated to tell a "cover" story about how the children merely got lost and really weren't up there on that mountain with aliens.

Hannah Jane eventually returned to her parents. We remained friends and shared secrets about the adventure we would tell no one else. I can only hint to you that while the authorities were nosing around, doing who knows what with the aliens, Hannah Jane and I still received messages from them from time to time. I guess I got enough of their blood in my system to open up my mind to many possibilities.

The John Croshaw mystery was answered as well. He was new to the area, from a county over from Transylvania, and had been hiking where he shouldn't have been when they caught him. He admitted to us that while under the influence of the aliens, he did have a sense that what he was doing was wrong, but he just could not do otherwise.

That explains the sparkle of confusion I had noticed in his eyes when I tried to talk him out of capturing me. He said he followed orders and did whatever was necessary to achieve the goals of his captors, but he was sorry for what he had done, even though he couldn't explain why he did it.

Hannah Jane continued her crush on him. I didn't mind, since I was grateful they were both alive. I heard that they did go out for a while. Then the inevitable happened: John Croshaw discovered there were other girls out there who couldn't resist him. He couldn't resist them either. Hannah Jane was not the kind of girl to share a man.

Jule and Gary Wayne stayed sweet on each other. My momma and daddy told the social workers that they could stay with us. But I always knew it was a matter of time before they married and moved up the mountain to a cabin with a view of those blue mountains.

Momma Opalona never did die. Leastwise, no one could ever recall her doing so. Last I heard, she moved away from town so she could enjoy her isolation higher up in the mountains.

Me? I decided I wanted to be a writer. I thought maybe I would want to teach at Brevard College when I grew up. But that was a long way off, and I knew there were still adventures for me, my friends, and maybe an alien or two. Stranger things have happened.

Like the day Gary Wayne came to me because he had an idea that I might like to accompany him on one last adventure.

"One more thing I gotta do," he announced.

My turn to follow him. So I said, "Me too," one more time.

We had hitchhiked for two days. Enough food for that and more in our backpacks. We slept in pastures and watched shooting stars at night. Of course, I wondered if maybe there weren't more than dying meteors in those rays of light that shot across the sky. On the third day, we had reached our destination.

The evening shadows had started to fall across the narrow cove down which we hiked, careful to keep in those shadows so as not to be detected.

"There." Gary Wayne pointed to a broken-down house that sat on the side of the road. Nothing distinguished it from the half dozen or so shanties that hugged the valley walls where we crept so cautiously. Nothing except the red Cushman motor scooter parked between a rusted Hudson sedan and a mint-green 1955 Ford that looked like it could have given a police patrol car a run for its money.

We made our special preparations, putting on the disguises we hoped would hide our identities from the present custodians of Gary Wayne's motor scooter. We both agreed that we owed Jule for the suggestion—that we wear disguises—which she grudgingly offered when Gary Wayne said he had his mind made up.

The smell of fresh-cooked supper, and the rush of diners from the yard and shed to the kitchen told us we could make our move.

We made it to the scooter without being noticed. I found a stick and let out the air from the back tires of the Ford. One look inside the Hudson told us no one had started that old car in years. We eased the motor scooter from its parking place and pointed it toward the road.

Now came the dangerous part. Gary Wayne kick-started it once. It sputtered. He tried it again. Nothing. By that time, our antics had caught the attention of the occupants of the house. Gary Wayne jumped on the starter again, and the machine sputtered, coughed, choked, and began a slow *put-put* that told us it was now or never. He feathered the throttle, and I hopped on the back. We were halfway up the hill, me pushing by now to get some more speed, when we could hear the engine of that Ford turn over and then, a moment later, the screams of its occupants saying things I do not care to repeat.

A clean getaway. We ditched our disguises where no one would find them. A day later, we pulled into Brevard, perched proudly aboard Gary Wayne's repossessed machine.

Jule met us with the daily newspaper. On the third page, a headline told the world of our accomplishment: WILD GIRLS STEAL MOTOR SCOOTER.

Yessir, those disguises Jule devised for us worked. "Ugliest girls I ever saw in my whole life," said the owner of the Ford.

Oh, yes, on the front page of that same paper, the headline read: ARMY SAYS ALIEN RUMOR A HOAX.

Wouldn't you know.

ALSO BY PATRICK BONE

A MELUNGEON WINTER

Two young friends—one white, the other black—become men when the father of one of them is wrongly accused and convicted of a murder. They turn to a feared Melungeon hermit whose wisdom and courage take the three of them on a jouney through Appalachia of the 1950s. With the assistance of a black holy woman who lives in a cave, and a 350-pound Texan who drives a tractor-trailer called *The Yellow Rose of Texas*, they uncover a plot involving bootleg whiskey, blackmail, and betrayal. Using humor, suspense, and folk legends, the author spins a tale of murder and friendship that rises above the prejudices of the times.

"A wonderful story . . . that satisfies at all levels. When I finished it I sat holding the book, wishing it wasn't over. . . . Patrick Bone is . . . an elegant writer with a true gift for language and dialect . . . a master at characterization."
—Lisa Lundquist, *Mystery News Review*

"I read it, absorbed it, and was awed by it . . . the characters came alive for me. I hated to see it end."
—Susan Johnson, MyShelf.com

"Like [Sharyn] McCrumb, he weaves his story with song and legend and . . . makes boyhood and an era come alive."
—a reviewer at PoisonedPen.com

Trade Paper 1-57072-144-0 $15.00
Hardcover 1-57072-143-2 $24.50

ALSO BY PATRICK BONE

BLOODY MARY

From its magical beginning in the time of Mary, Queen of Scots, an evil spell corrupts the lives of all who touch it. Only children believe the legend:

Say "Blood Mary" in the mirror thirteen times, and you will become the monster.

When Amanda Terry finds a mysterious mirror hidden in a box in the attic of her new, "haunted" home, she unknowlingly releases the spirit of Bloody Mary. When Amanda's stepsister, Juli, succombs to the power of the magic mirror, no one believes Amanda. No one helps her when she tries to resolve the dilemma she now faces. No one, that is, except an odd assortment: her favorite teacher, an eerie storyteller, a playful ghost, the neighborhood witch, and the all-time greatest solver of mysteries—the public library.

"*Bloody Mary* is the best . . . children's book I have read in a long time. It ranks up there with stories from when I was a child that kept me up nights. Any kid will love it and will be telling the story for years to come around campfires and sleepovers. . . ."

—a fan at amazon.com

"The child within me came out to play."
—Frieda Weeks, Greeneville, Tennessee

"As a parent, I appreciate the fact that my children can read a scary story that doesn't use gore as a crutch. . . . I especially liked Amanda's relationship with her father."
—Jeff McCord, *Rogersville Review*

Trade Paper 1-57072-093-2 $9.95

WE'RE BLOWING THE LID OFF THESE MYSTERIES COMING SOON:

HAUNTING REFRAIN

by Ellis Vidler

A body in a lake, a shooting in a mountain park. A murderer roams the Piedmont, and photographer Kate McGuire is on the list. It's up to her to find the killer and save herself.

When injury forces San Antonio policewoman Rachael Grant to return home, she learns the family guest ranch, Tumbleweeds, has been sold. Her inept cousin is accused of killing the new owner, and Rachael finds herself searching for the real murderer as well as the real meaning of home.

HOME IS WHERE THE MURDER IS

by Carolyn Rogers

JUSTICE BETRAYED

by Daniel Bailey

Entangling the countryside in a confusing mass of lies and deceit, an insidious governmental conspiracy creeps across South Carolina's Lowcountry like rancorous kudzu, leaving death and a betrayal of justice along its path.

SILVER DAGGER MYSTERIES